THE CURSE
OF ZOHREH

THE CURSE OF ZOHREH

Book Two in The Chronicles of El Jisal

a fantasy novel by

Sophie Masson

RANDOM HOUSE AUSTRALIA

Random House Australia Pty Ltd
20 Alfred Street, Milsons Point, NSW 2061
http://www.randomhouse.com.au

Sydney   New York   Toronto
London   Auckland   Johannesburg

First published by Random House Australia 2005

National Library of Australia
Cataloguing-in-Publication Entry

    Masson, Sophie, 1959– .
    The curse of Zohreh.

    For secondary students.
    ISBN 1 74166 072 6.

    I. Title.

A823.3

Cover and internal illustrations by Xavier Masson-Leach
Cover and internal design by Sandra Nobes
Typeset in Bembo by Midland Typesetters
Printed and bound by Griffin Press, Netley, South Australia

10 9 8 7 6 5 4 3 2 1

For Eva, with many thanks

PARSARI

Shideh

Jumana

MESOMIA

AMEERAT

MASRIKHAN

FARAONA

Umalkur

Narrow
Sea

Gulf of
Parsari

SHEBANAM

RIYALDAW

Shining
Sea

AMEERAT
and its Neighbours

N ←——→ S

Every Night and every Morn,
Some to Misery are born.
Every Morn and every Night,
Some are born to sweet delight,
Some are Born to sweet delight,
Some are born to Endless Night.

From *Auguries of Innocence* by William Blake (1803)

Prologue

Zohreh the Akamenian was far from being an ordinary old lady. Everyone was agreed on that. She was small and light-boned as a bird, and had bright blue eyes whose sharpness belied her age. The matriarch of the Melkior clan had fought all her long life for the good of her family. Despite the early death of her beloved husband, Darius, with hard work and talent she had made the Melkior clan one of the richest and most respected merchant families in all of Parsari. She kept a hawk-eye on accounts, on inventories, on the quality of the goods. And she only bought the best: the finest cottons from Alhind, the most beautiful brocaded silks from Radentengan, the sheerest gauzes from the furthest corners of the Rummiyan Empire, the loveliest gilded batiks from Jayangan. She had customers amongst the rich and powerful all over Dawtarn el 'Jisal, and beyond, and was received with respect in many palaces and mansions.

So no-one in her family even dreamt of trying to stop her when she announced her decision to sail on the next trade trip to Jumana, chief port city of the Al Aksara principality of Ameerat. She had, she said sternly, discovered troubling irregularities in the trade with Ameerat which needed to be sorted out personally. She would be back, God willing, in a few weeks. No, she did not need her son or daughter-in-law to accompany her – they needed to look after the business at home. She did not even want to take bodyguards, because she wanted no fuss, but in the end was persuaded to take one of the family's most loyal and fierce retainers, Orman the Cimmerian.

She also took the family's most prized possession, the Talisman of the Star – a tiny wooden box containing a thin strip of linen which had once been a band from a little prince's swaddling-cloth. It had been brought back hundreds of years ago by their highpriestly ancestor, Melkior, the Magvanda of the Stars, from a country far to the east. The Talisman of the Star had always helped to protect the family, and now it, and Orman's sword, would protect Zohreh on this dangerous journey.

Zohreh cut off her hair and disguised herself as a man. In Jumana she would pose as a corrupt employee, Amin. That way, she would find out what was happening quicker – and it would be less dangerous than coming as herself.

As soon as the ship docked in Jumana, Zohreh began her investigation, Orman at her side. She discovered almost at once that her suspicions were justified. The Melkior clan was being defrauded by the Ameerat end of the business. Abbas and Salman, two of the workers employed in the family's office in Jumana, were diverting bales of cloth. They were doing it just one bale at a time, every so often, and not the most valuable stuff, so as not to attract undue attention.

This they learnt as Orman stood over the men, sword at their throats. And they learnt even more from the panic-stricken cheats: that this was no minor fraud, no isolated occurrence, but part of a massive pattern of theft and extortion on the docks of Jumana. Abbas and Salman had been told that if they did not steal the bales, not only would they be killed, but their families as well; they were then given a small amount of money to sweeten the deal. And they were not the only ones, the two men cried, tongues loosened by fear and perhaps, too, by the relief of finally getting it off their chests. Orman and Amin should go and ask all the other shipping agents, they said. They'd soon see they were telling the truth. But when the supposed Amin asked them harshly who was behind it all, they refused to speak.

Zohreh was furious, and determined to expose the criminal behind this web of cheating and extortion. It was not only for her own clan, now; she was afraid this cheating would undermine and even destroy the rich trade between Parsari and Al Aksara. She would find out who it was, and then go and see the Prince of Ameerat and lay the results before him.

But one had to go carefully in the lands of Al Aksara. People here could be fiendishly proud, all too ready to be insulted. So Zohreh wove patient webs, listening, watching, keeping her nose close to the ground. What Abbas and Salman had claimed was true: there was an underlying pattern of small irregularities which put together amounted to a gigantic conspiracy to defraud the foreign merchants of Jumana.

Little by little, by dint of patient investigation and careful thinking, Zohreh came to an inescapable but frightening conclusion: the mastermind of this conspiracy was none other than the head of port security, the very rich, very arrogant nobleman Lord Kassim bin Saad al-Farouk. As well as being in charge of the port, Al-Farouk was a distant cousin of the Prince, and ran his own private army. He was not one to be taken on lightly, or accused frivolously, if you valued your life. But Zohreh was determined not to be beaten.

To protect herself, she sent a letter back to her family in Parsari, setting out what she had already learnt, and what she suspected. Then she took her courage in both hands, placed the Talisman of the Star carefully in the folds of her turban for protection, and set out with Orman to beard Kassim al-Farouk in his den.

The nobleman lived in a magnificent estate, far from the stink and noise of the port. His white mansion, surrounded by lovely walled gardens, covered a large acreage. Within its grounds he kept chained leopards, monkeys, peacocks, and a host of gorgeous birds in filigreed aviaries. Roses from Masrikhan, lilies from Parsari and jasmine from Alhind filled the air with their glorious perfume. Room after room was filled with the most beautiful carpets, curtains made of billowing gauze, and decorations in real gold and silver, inlaid with precious stones. The sight of it all filled Zohreh with a deep anger. This man needed nothing, yet in his greed he wanted more. He must be stopped.

Kassim al-Farouk had agreed to see them because he knew well the name of Zohreh the Akamenian and he was curious to meet her agent, Amin. Tall, beginning to run to fat, with a hard face, a big black beard, and the yellow-brown, unblinking eyes of a bird of prey, Kassim al-Farouk was a ruthless and clever man in the prime of life. Surrounded by his retainers, his imposing bulk reflected in the tall carved mirror behind him, he greeted his visitors in a civil but distant fashion, as befitted his noble rank. He called for mint tea and sugared pastries and for a time he and Amin, with the silent Orman standing behind him, conversed in a genteel fashion about their respective countries.

Then Amin leant forward to the big nobleman and whispered, 'Your highness, there is possibly something we need to talk of, privately — it is about what is happening at the port — there are opportunities — things I would like to tell you about.'

Kassim's yellow eyes fastened on the old man's blue ones. Kassim had a disconcerting stare, blank of emotion. Inwardly Zohreh shuddered a little, but soon mastered herself. After a short silence Kassim waved at his retainers, nonchalantly telling them to leave the room, and also at Orman, who after a look at Amin, also retired.

'Now, old man,' the nobleman said in a quiet, dangerous voice, 'what is it you wanted to tell me?'

Amin swallowed, ducked his head, stammered, 'My lord, I wish to say — to say that — I think — think we might come to an arrangement.' Zohreh was not really afraid; she was acting the part of a man who could be corrupted. Nevertheless, she could not help a flutter in her chest. This was the most perilous moment of her life. Would the man fall into her trap?

Kassim's eyes narrowed. 'An arrangement, Amin?'

'My lord, the old woman who runs the business — Zohreh of the Melkior clan — she is a hard woman, grasping. And a dirty infidel, too. I have long suffered at her hands.'

'Yet you have not long worked for her.' Kassim's voice was flat.

'You are well informed, my lord.'

'It is my business to be so. Cut the nonsense. Tell me what you want to say.'

'My lord, I know – I know there is to be a very valuable shipment sent to Jumana, very soon, from the old woman. The finest silks, and gold brocade – worth a prince's ransom, sir. I thought perhaps that –'

'Why have you come to me with this, old man?' Kassim's hand shot out, and he grasped Amin's wrist in a grip of steel. 'Why have you come here?'

'Sir –' Amin's eyes fluttered rapidly, '– it is just that I – that I admire you so greatly, and that I believe you are – you are more deserving than my wicked, domineering, infidel mistress.'

'Are you offering me her cargo?' Kassim's eyes did not flicker; his grasp on Amin's wrist did not slacken. But his tongue darted out to lick at his thin lips. Amin nodded.

Kassim gave a grunt. 'Her entire cargo? That would be too obvious.'

Zohreh's heart leapt. He had fallen for it completely. Such is the nature of all-consuming greed.

'Accidents can be arranged,' Amin murmured. 'Shipwrecks – acts of piracy – sadly, these do happen.'

For the first time, Kassim smiled. 'You are an evil old man,' he said. 'Dear, dear, and to think that a greybeard can think such thoughts! You interest me, Amin the Parsarian. What do you want out of this?'

'Revenge and reward,' said Amin.

Kassim looked deep into his eyes. He nodded. 'Very well. You will come here again tomorrow and give me all the details of this cargo and when it is due to arrive. We will then make arrangements.' He paused. 'You will find me generous. But you will not find me stupid. You have betrayed your mistress, and everyone knows that a traitor cannot be trusted. So beware, Amin the Parsarian, if you even think of doublecrossing me.'

Zohreh was thrilled by the success of her mission. Tomorrow morning, she thought, she would go and seek an audience with the Prince and lay everything before him. He couldn't fail to act.

What she had neglected to take into account was that Kassim had spies amongst the networks of little shops and offices that dealt with the trade of foreign merchants. And one of these, a man named Ali, had gone to visit his good friends Abbas and Salman, only to discover that they had been dismissed. Asking around, he found it had been a very sudden dismissal indeed. Knowing his master liked to be aware of everything that was happening around the port, he reported this titbit of information to Kassim.

Kassim listened to Ali with a set face and murder in his heart. He instantly put two and two together and knew that Amin was seeking to entrap him. The old man is a spy for Zohreh, he thought, and might well bring me down if he is able to get to the Prince with his information. There is no time to lose.

Zohreh was asleep when Kassim's men burst into her tiny room. Though she was still wearing her man's

Kassim did not understand all that Zohreh was saying but he knew enough Parsarian for a long, cold shiver to ripple down his back as the curses rolled over him. For a second he hesitated, almost deciding in his fear to spare her life. Then, he saw clearly the certain fate that would await him if he did not kill her and she told the Prince of Ameerat all she had learnt. With a ferocious yell, he swung the sword down and across, and decapitated Zohreh in mid-sentence. Her head flew across the room, her lips still seemingly uttering curses for a flicker of a second after her death; her body slumped to the ground, blood gushing out of her neck. The witch was dead. Dead! She would never trouble him again.

He called to his guards to drag the body out and leave it in the guardroom. Then he went, in disguise, to where Zohreh had been staying. He searched her room from top to bottom, and took away all the notes she had made and all the information she had compiled. He also found the Talisman, wrapped in the turban. He had no idea what it was – to him it was just a little box with a filthy bit of rag inside it. He would have destroyed it along with the rest of Zohreh's possessions but something told him it must be valuable. After all, the box itself was a most beautiful little thing, even if the rag was disgusting, and why would the old woman have brought it with her from Parsari if it wasn't some kind of good-luck charm? Perhaps the luck of the

robe and a hooded cloak, she had taken off her turban, and with it, the Talisman of the Star, still nestled in its folds. She had no time and no opportunity to seize it, and though she fought like a lion against her attackers, as did her retainer Orman, it was hopeless. There were too many assailants, and they were all heavily armed. Orman soon lay dead on the floor, while Amin was dragged off to Kassim's mansion and flung at the nobleman's feet, before the tall carved mirror in the room where he had received them earlier that day.

'So, old man,' said Kassim, 'you thought to trick me. Me, Kassim the Great! You thought to cheat and lie to me. Well, my friend, before you die you will tell me why. You will tell me why your mistress sent you to do this.'

Zohreh knew she was finished. She did not have the protection of the Talisman of the Star. She knew she would die, alone and in suffering, in this foreign land, at the hands of a wicked man.

Rising to her feet, she said proudly, 'Know you are speaking not to Amin the Parsarian, but to Zohreh the Akamenian, descendant of the great Magvanda of the Stars, Melkior. Know, wicked Kassim, that your days are numbered, for already a letter is making its way across the gulf to Parsari and in it, everything is told. Know that the vengeance of the clan of Melkior will descend on you, and that you will be punished, no matter what you do to me, or what you have done to my faithful Orman.'

Kassim stood as if frozen. Then he strode forward and grabbed Zohreh. He pulled hard at the wispy beard — most of it came off in his hand, and he saw it had been glued on. He would have yanked at the robe, but Zohreh sprang back. 'Do not touch me, Kassim. Do not touch me, or it will be the worse for you.'

Kassim regarded her with the eyes of a leopard watching his prey. A cruel smile curved his lips. 'So, Zohreh the Akamenian. You think thus to trap me. You fool. Have you forgotten? You are not of our faith. You are an infidel in the sacred heartland of the Mujisals. It is considered a crime in our country to come here dressed as a man, when you are a weak woman. Worse yet, you have dressed as a devout Mujisal, as one who has been to make the pilgrimage to the great House of Light. And I am sure that I can find witnesses to agree that you have been heard talking to various men in the port district, seeking to convert them to your filthy fire-worshipping religion. Any judge can sentence you to immediate death for this offence. And so it shall be done, for I, Kassim al-Farouk, as head of port security, have legal authority conferred on me.' He picked up his sword. 'Your cargo will be confiscated, your crew banished, your ship seized. And no member of your family will ever be able to set foot in Ameerat again, on pain of death.'

'You forget my letter, Kassim.' She faced the nobleman bravely, coldly, as he advanced with sword in hand. 'You forget that it will make its way to Parsari.'

'Who will pay attention to your letter once the royal family of Parsari has been appraised of the fact that the Melkior clan are a tribe of traitors who cannot be trusted? I have fast ships and dedicated men, Zohreh; my message will get to Parsari much faster than yours.'

It was then Zohreh knew she had lost everything. In the winter of her years, she had foolishly brought ruin not only upon herself, but on her whole family. She called on all her courage, and her faith. She prayed passionately in her heart to her God, Lord Akamenia, Flame of the World, begging for forgiveness for her sins, and asking for him and all his angels to protect her family, now they had lost the Talisman of the Star. She asked his prophet, the Truthteller, to arm her soul for what she must do now.

Then she turned to face Kassim. In a cold, harsh voice that rose into a weird, high chant, she began to curse him in her own language. She cursed him and his family down through all the generations, calling for eternal fire to destroy him, for soul-fire to torment him, for his very name to be blackened and tainted throughout the whole of history. It would not end with Kassim, she shrieked. Death by fire would await each firstborn child, on his or her fifteenth birthday, till the family had paid in full for what Kassim was about to do.

Melkiors would be his now. Back at the palace, he wrapped it carefully in several layers of silk and placed it in the hollow spine of a book in his vast library, where it would be well hidden.

It all happened exactly as Kassim had hoped. The Prince of Ameerat viewed Zohreh's body, still in its male Mujisal disguise, and talked to several men, all Kassim's agents, who swore on the Holy Book of Light that the infidel foreigner had been trying to convert them. He was saddened. He had liked Zohreh. She must have gone mad, he decided. He ordered that her and Orman's bodies be burnt and the ashes sent back to Parsari, with a letter explaining what she had been guilty of. He allowed Kassim to seize Zohreh's ship and all the cargo that had not yet been sold, as well as the money Zohreh had already made on that trip. He also wrote to the Governor of Shideh, the city Zohreh had come from, informing him that the Melkior clan was no longer welcome in Ameerat.

The Emperor of Parsari, on hearing what had happened, ordered that Zohreh's family must be made to pay for her crime, and imposed such heavy penalties on them that they lost all their money and standing. Zohreh's letter was useless, for by the time it reached the family they were already in deep disgrace. Zohreh's son knew that his mother's accusations against the great nobleman Kassim al-Farouk would simply not be listened to. The Melkior clan slid into debt-ridden obscurity. Eventually, they had to abandon their grand mansion in Shideh, never to return. They settled in the poor, remote town of Sholeh, in the grim mountains to the north, where they hid their origins and eked out a hard-scrabble existence as farmers and small traders. They knew nothing of the curse Zohreh had called down on Kassim and his family.

Besides, even if they'd known, they would have thought the curse had been ineffective, for Kassim al-Farouk prospered greatly after the death of his enemy. If the Melkior clan's luck was connected with the ownership of the Talisman of the Star, then it had certainly transferred to the clan of al-Farouk. Kassim hardly ever thought of Zohreh and her curse, and when he did, would smile mockingly to himself. That old fire-breather had just been a stupid old woman. And besides, his firstborn had been long past his fifteenth birthday when she placed the curse. It meant nothing. It was without any power at all.

And then came the day when a mysterious fire started in Kassim's bedchamber in the middle of the night. His son, Ghazi, pulled him out, but he was already far too badly burnt to survive. With his last breath, his eyes wide open and staring on a vision of unimaginable horror, Kassim groaned, brokenly, 'She did it – the witch did it – the curse of Zohreh – the curse, my son – eternal fire to descend on us – guard your first-born – beware – beware – beware the fifteenth birthday.' And then he was dead, before Ghazi could ask him any more.

No-one ever worked out exactly what had caused the fire in Kassim's bedchamber that day; indeed, the manner of his horrible death was completely hushed up. Ghazi made a few discreet investigations and found out from one of the guards who Zohreh was, and what had happened between her and his father. Ghazi had no children, as yet, but he had recently married, and it would surely not be long before his wife had a baby. Was the child doomed before he or she was even born?

Now Ghazi was not at all like his father. He was horrified by what had been done to Zohreh. He would have liked to make it up to her family, but he lacked the courage to do so. He was reluctant to court disgrace by trying to right the wrong that had been done. Devoutly hoping the curse had somehow been accomplished with the terrible death of his father, he kept silent.

It was a fatal silence. He did have children, and his firstborn, a beautiful young girl, was struck by lightning coming out of a clear sky, on the very day of her fifteenth birthday, and died, horribly burnt and disfigured. Ghazi was inconsolable, and died of a broken heart several months later. On his deathbed, he told his oldest son Faisal about the curse of Zohreh, and begged him to try and find Zohreh's family and make reparation.

Faisal tried hard to find the Melkior clan but nobody was able to tell him where they had gone. They had disappeared. When his own child was born he waited in terror for the curse to hit him and took every possible precaution, but the child passed his fifteenth birthday without mishap and grew to be a healthy and lively young man. Perhaps the curse had exhausted itself, with the deaths of Kassim and his grandaughter?

Curses were notoriously erratic, even those like Zohreh's. If the curse had been that of a supernatural being, like a Jinn's, it would have been much more reliable. But a human witch or sorcerer, however powerful, could not guarantee the hundred per cent effectiveness of a curse. Or so Faisal hoped.

Still, he passed on the story to his son, who passed it on to his son, for it was better to be prepared.

One

'This has to stop, my son!' Shayk Abdullah al-Farouk furiously waved a scrap of paper in the air. 'What is the meaning of this?'

His son, Khaled, stared back impassively. 'You weren't meant to see it, Father. The servants took it from my room without asking.'

'That's not the point!' roared the Shayk, his usually kindly eyes almost popping out of his head with frustration. 'You've not been eating properly, not been sleeping properly, and wandering about in a daze for months – now this!' He read out loud from the piece of paper: 'In demons' fire, the soul twists – going into the fire – forever fire – fire and flame – the realm of fire.' In a paroxysm of rage, he threw the paper on the floor. He pounded the floor with his walking-stick. 'Have you gone mad, Khaled? You used to write such beautiful poetry – now all you write is this crazy, devilish gibberish.'

Khaled had gone quite white. 'Father,' he said quietly, 'in ten days' time I'll be turning fifteen.'

Abdullah closed his eyes briefly. When he spoke again his voice was softer, gentler. 'Don't you think I know that, Khaled? My own brother, the first born, died on his fifteenth birthday in a terrible fire at the bazaar. I am well aware of the curse, my son. But you know that we have taken steps to prevent it happening, through prayer and fasting, and the protection of holy men – unlike my father, who ignored the curse as a mere superstition. And we . . .'

'Father,' interrupted Khaled, 'do you know that my birthday will mark exactly the hundredth anniversary of Zohreh's curse?' Seeing his father's puzzled expression, he went on, 'I've been reading up about these kinds of curses. They are always erratic, and their power seems to wane considerably after a hundred years, though not end completely. Some writers think that on the hundredth anniversary the curse is at its most powerful and dangerous since the time it was first pronounced. And that means me, Father. It will be in its full force against me.'

It was Abdullah's turn to go white. He limped to his son's bed and sat down. 'Perhaps – perhaps it's not true. Perhaps they're just guessing.'

'Perhaps,' said Khaled. 'But Father, we can't just hope for the best. We've got to do something about it, permanently. Not only for my sake, but because what was done to Zohreh all those years ago was horrible, Father. It was shameful. Kassim tainted our family honour. And that shame needs to be wiped right away.'

'But you know we tried to find the family, and failed.'

'I know, Father. But maybe we've been looking for them the wrong way.' He picked up the scrap of paper. 'You see, what I was actually trying to do with this is compose a password. I thought of it only yesterday.'

Abdullah stared at him in utter astonishment. 'A *password*?'

'Yes, a password, to enter other worlds . . . It came to me yesterday that perhaps, as Zohreh was from a faith that venerates fire as the symbol of God, and as fire of some kind has been the cause of death in those of us who were killed by the curse, then it's in the realm of fire that we must seek answers: to end the curse, and to find Zohreh's family. And you know who comes from the realm of fire.'

'The Jinn,' whispered Abdullah, his eyes fixed on his son's handsome face. The Jinn, supernatural beings created out of fire by God, are shape-shifters whose magical powers range from the vast to the modest, and who can be evil, good, or in-between.

'That's right, the Jinn! And more specifically, the most powerful spirits amongst them, the wild Desert-Jinn, who are closest of all to the fiery element.'

Abdullah shook his head. 'My son, I'm not sure you know what you're saying. The Jinn are unpredictable at the best of times, especially those from the desert. They are not human, remember; we don't always understand them. Tame House-Jinns are one thing. Those wild ones you speak of – why, to meet them unawares is bad enough, but to deliberately seek them out, password or no password, is sheer madness.' He gulped. 'Have you thought that calling on the aid of a Jinn might be a way the curse could come down on you – what if an evil Jinn should decide to burn you?'

Khaled nodded slowly. He took his father's hand. 'I have thought of that, Father. I promise I will be careful. I will write the sacred word "adhubilah" on a wristband and wear it always. That has always been a good protection against the evil ones amongst the Jinn. And I will carry a vial of holy zummiyah water with me. I do not think the wicked Jinn will dare to hurt me. And I may persuade a good Jinn to help me. Father, will you give me your blessing in this undertaking?'

'Oh, Khaled, my dear, dear son,' said Abdullah, tears in his eyes, 'you are a brave, clever child. You have thought of good protections. But I still fear that these things may not be enough to protect you.'

'Father, time is short. I must at least try. I cannot wait for the curse to fell me, or not. I've lived in enough fear as it is. Can't you see, I must do something myself.'

Abdullah's heart swelled with pride. Khaled reminded him so much of his dear, dead wife Leyla – in his looks, in his intelligence, his character, determination and unusual insights. Abdullah had been well into middle age when he married her, and crippled already by the riding accident that had smashed his left leg. He had been amazed that she loved him, and heartbroken when she died when Khaled was only two. But she lived again in her son. It was typical of Leyla's child to want to attempt what others would be too frightened to even think about. And why not? You couldn't change the past, but maybe you could change the future. He sighed deeply. 'I do understand, my dearest Khaled. And I do give you my blessing. But I have only ever known one person who has consorted with the wild Jinn and lived to tell the tale.'

'Oh, Father, who is it? Perhaps this person could advise me.' Khaled's dark eyes were filled with sudden hope.

Abdullah clapped his hands. 'You're quite right! He could most likely advise you very well. We grew up together, Husam al-Din and I. He came from a noble family, but they were poor. Husam had to earn his living as a swordsman, and eventually he became the Chief Executioner for the Sultan of Jayangan, way across the eastern ocean. I have kept in touch with him over the years, and I know he is now retired. I will get a message to him at once.' He picked up the telephone on Khaled's bedside table, and dialled. 'This is Shayk Abdullah al-Farouk. I want a telegram sent immediately to an address in Jayangan. Mark it as extremely urgent . . .'

They received Husam al-Din's reply the very next day. He would set off straightaway and would be in Ameerat within three days. And he would bring with him someone who would greatly help in their task. 'She is a free Desert-Jinn, a red-headed songstress by the name of Kareen Amar. Forget about passwords, they aren't necessary in this undertaking! No, I haven't enslaved her, dear friend,' he had scrawled, 'she chooses to be with humans.'

Two

A century after the terrible events that had claimed the life of Zohreh the Akamenian, the Melkior clan had melted away to almost nothing. Misfortune had followed misfortune. Hiding under another name, not daring to even practise their religion in public, they were poor and lived in utter obscurity in remote Sholeh. But they never forgot Zohreh, and her cruel fate. Her ashes, enclosed in a silken sachet, rested in a little box which stood on the altar of the family's household shrine; the last letter she had written was locked away in a secret drawer; and the sad story of her death, and the loss of the Talisman, was told through all the generations. They did not know about the curse that Zohreh had called down on the al-Farouk family, for the al-Farouks had kept it very quiet indeed.

The youngest member of the family, thirteen-year-old Soheila, knew the story inside out, like all her kin. As far back as she could remember, she had wept about it, like the others. But with the sadness had also come a huge anger. She burned with rage at the thought that the al-Farouks had got away scot-free with the crime. Their doings were reported every now and then in the papers, as Abdullah al-Farouk was not only very rich but also an important man. He was one of the top councillors to the Prince of Ameerat. How could the descendants of a murderer, a liar and a thief prosper so spectacularly, while the descendants of his victim lived a life of struggle and poverty so far removed from their previous luxury? It wasn't fair that the Melkior clan was so reduced and dependent on the goodwill of others, while the al-Farouks did just as they pleased, in ease and comfort. She simmered with the injustice of it.

It was a few months ago that the idea had first come to her. She had woken from a vivid dream in which she'd been following a hooded figure through a bright desert — yellow sand, blue sky — and then suddenly, there was a white palace, shimmering in the light. She heard a voice, whispering, 'It is time. You must come.' The hooded figure beckoned to her so she went through the palace's imposing gates, and there, suddenly, her heart began to beat so fast that it woke her up. She was bathed in sweat, her heart was still beating fast, but she knew at once what the dream meant. She had to stop weeping and raging over Zohreh's fate, and with it, the fate of her family. A new urgency drove her. The figure — it must be Zohreh — had said it was time. She had to go to the desert principality of Ameerat, find the al-Farouks in their white palace, and make them pay, in blood and tears.

Soheila was not by nature a vengeful person. But she had more than a trace of her ancestor's defiant spirit and determination. The rest of her family believed that it was better to keep your head low and your mouth shut, both as members of a disgraced clan and as adherents to a minority religion that had been more and more persecuted in recent times. Soheila could not live like that. She wanted to hold her head high, to look people in the eye, not creep along like a kicked dog, hoping no-one would notice her.

Though her heart was full of excitement, she did not breathe a word of her plans to her parents or her older brother. They were all too meek, too ground-down by life, to even try to rebel. Her mother, Tara, was an invalid. She couldn't walk any more, and spent her days embroidering fine shawls for the few wealthy women of Sholeh. Her father, Atash, had taken refuge long ago in sweet wine. A gentle, trusting dreamer, he had tried many times to revive the family fortunes, but had failed. Earning money for the family was left to Tara, with her sewing, and Soheila's brother, Aslarn, who worked in their uncle's small store in Sholeh.

Soheila did not yet earn her living. She went to school and worked on weekends helping out at her uncle's shop. It was Tara's wish for her daughter not to work full time, for she was afraid no man would want to marry her if she grew old before her time, working her fingers to the bone. Soheila was a beautiful girl, slight and delicate, with black hair, olive skin, and startling blue-green eyes that she had inherited from Zohreh herself. And she was clever, graceful and musical; she might well make a good marriage one of these days. She might even marry into a wealthy family, or at least one of the merchants of Sholeh, if she played her cards right. That was Tara's dream for her daughter. But it wasn't Soheila's for herself, not at all.

Once, she might have said she hoped to be a great singer, but music did not interest her any more. All she thought about was revenge on the al-Farouks. Soheila loved her parents and brother dearly, but she wished that they would stand up and look fate full in the face, and spit in its cruel eye. Human beings were not puppets. They could act on their own. They could take their fate in their own hands. And so she would. She would redress the stain on the family honour. She would do as Zohreh wanted.

Over a few months, she researched possibilities, taught herself some Aksaran, and learnt as much as she could about Ameeratan ways, history and customs. She made her plans. She would leave Sholeh and travel across the sea to Ameerat. She would go disguised as a Parsarian boy with an Ameeratan mother, and find employment in some capacity in the al-Farouks' palace.

She would try to find out what had happened to the Talisman. And then she would strike when she was ready – hard, without mercy. There had to be a merciless death to avenge Zohreh's. Tragedy had to strike the al-Farouks, to pay for the tragedy that had struck the Melkiors. She had to close the circle.

Soheila had saved the small amount of money her uncle gave her for her weekend work. Her mother had refused to allow her to put it into the family finances – Soheila was to keep it for her eventual wedding, she said. It would be enough to get to the port of Shideh, to buy some second-hand boys' clothes, a bit of food, and find passage on one of the wooden sambuks that plied the gulf.

She waited for the right moment to leave. Finally, a day came. Her parents were out of the house because Aslarn had picked them up in his rickety old car to take them to the hot springs where her mother went often in the vain hope of a cure. Soheila had pleaded off the trip by claiming she needed to study. As soon as the car had disappeared in a cloud of dust up the road, Soheila gathered together her few things and wrote a brief note to her parents saying that she was going to seek her fortune and that they were not to worry about her. She was about to leave the house when she suddenly thought of something. The Talisman was lost to her, but maybe Zohreh's ashes would help to protect her, and help her to stay true to her task. So she took Zohreh's ashes, in their silken sachet, out of the box and carefully put them in her clothes, next to her heart. She breathed a silent prayer, asking Akamenia to protect her family, and left.

She only looked back once, when she was almost at the end of the street. The little two-roomed mud-brick house crouching amongst its fellows on the dusty road already looked to her eyes like it belonged in the past. She closed her mind to the pictures of her child-hood – of her mother, frail even then, but walking, smiling as she held her in her arms, and her father, still hopeful back then, throwing her up and down while she crowed with delight. She must not become home-sick, must not regret, must not doubt. She must be strong. She must cast away all soft feelings. She must only focus on the need for revenge and justice.

She walked a few blocks to the bus stop, where there were quite a few people waiting. The bus would take her to Shirinah, a bigger town some distance away, and there she would catch a connecting all-night bus to Shideh, the faraway port city where ships left for Ameerat. She told idly curious neighbours she saw while waiting for the bus that she was going to pick up something for her uncle in Shirinah. No-one thought anything of it. She had gone to Shirinah by herself before.

It was only an hour to Shirinah. Someone jammed a crate of chickens next to her at one stop, and then baskets overflowing with vegetables, but she did not mind. She gazed out of the window as the bus lurched and jolted along the bumpy road, and her heart was filled with a fierce excitement. She was doing it at last! Her fate was in God's hands now.

In Shirinah, she made straight for a second-hand clothes shop she had noticed on her last visit there. No-one knew her in Shirinah, but because the shop-keeper looked mildly curious about the fact she was buying boys' clothing, she spun him a soft-voiced story about a nonexistent little brother. Her sweet, innocent-seeming face and modest attitude put to rest any doubts he might have had.

Clutching her parcel of clothes, she made her way to a nearby park, which was little frequented at that time of the day. She hid behind a bushy shrub, and quickly changed into the loose grey tunic and pants she had bought. She put Zohreh's ashes in the pocket of the tunic, over her heart. Then she took scissors she had brought from home and roughly hacked off her shining hair close to her scalp, rubbed some dirt into her face, and rolled her old clothes into a ball and shoved them under the bush. She took out her small pocket mirror and looked critically at herself: yes, she would pass as a boy. A small, slight, beardless boy, it was true, but a boy. She had studied the way boys walked and talked, and she would take care never to show any girlish feelings. Her studies in music would come in useful, for she had trained her voice and her register was wide. She would speak in the light, pleasant tones of a tenor, and no-one would know she was a girl.

She experienced a strange, exhilarating yet hollow feeling standing there in the dusty park, knowing that everything she'd known till then — even her own self — would have to be left behind. Soheila the Akamenian had vanished. In her place stood Payem the Parsarian, street urchin, who was off to seek his fortune in wealthy Ameerat, like so many young Parsarians had done before him. From now on, not only would she think like him and speak like him — she would *be* him.

Three

'Oh, no, no, no, it will not do at all,' said Kareen Amar, shaking her head most decisively. The red-haired Jinn stalked away from the bazaar stall, her motley collection of jewellery jangling, her ramrod-straight back expressing great disapproving disappointment. Husam al-Din sighed, shrugged and, pacifying the cranky carpet dealer with a crumpled banknote and a muttered excuse, set off, black robes billowing in the sea breeze, after his unpredictable friend. The long, wearisome trudge through the famous Market Fair of Kapalau had long since lost any allure it might once have had. Famous it might be, but in the end, it was a bazaar like all others – hot, dusty, noisy and unbearably crowded. Already, Husam missed his quiet beach, and his fishing line, and his black woollen tent, back home at Siluman. If it had not been for the great affection he bore his old friend back in Ameerat, he would almost have felt like cutting short the whole enterprise.

Kareen Amar had heard there was a flying carpet being offered for sale in the market – not an ordinary flying carpet, but a rare thing indeed, for it had been made by one of the legendary Carpet Enchantresses of Mesomia. 'We must go to Kapalau and find it,' she had said firmly. 'It will transport us to Ameerat much more quickly than any other thing.' And she hadn't listened to any of Husam's protests about planes being perfectly all right. Truth to tell, Husam didn't like planes much, but flying carpets made him even more nervous, after a bad experience with one over the deserts of Ameerat, when he was a child. They could be as unpredictable as horses, possessing spirits of their own, not obedient slaves like machines.

Kareen Amar had merely snorted at Husam's protestations. 'This one is made by a Carpet Enchantress,' she said. 'It will be good and reliable. I can guarantee that.'

The carpet was not for sale openly. It was contraband and had to be sold in secret. And Kareen Amar did not know where in the market she'd find it. Hence the trudge, and the questioning of stallholders.

Husam became aware that the Jinn was gesturing triumphantly at him from across one of the crowded aisles. Her eyes glowed, like Jinns' eyes do when they are deeply moved in some way. 'I told you that I, Kareen Amar, would find it, no matter how well it was hidden from plain sight,' she said smugly, when Husam joined her. 'And so I have, my friend. Come with me. You will see what I have seen and will regret your lack of faith in Kareen Amar!'

'Oh, Kareen,' sighed Husam, 'I never thought you –' But his words fell on deaf ears, for Kareen Amar was already shouldering her heedless way through the pressing crowds, and it was all he could do to keep up with her. Excitement was beginning to build in him. Much as he distrusted flying carpets generally, it was true to say that if this one was really made by a Mesomian Carpet Enchantress, then it would be a real treasure. Such carpets were rare at the best of times, and even more so now that the great and ancient Guild of Carpet Enchantresses had been practically destroyed by Haroun bin Said al-Alakah, better known as The Vampire, the wicked tyrant of Mesomia. Its remaining members had scattered into the impenetrable Southern Marshlands of Mesomia, where they lived in great secrecy and hardship. You almost never saw a carpet from their looms these days, and when you did, it was immediately snapped up and jealously guarded by its new owners. The rumour was that this one was a prototype, made by one of the younger members of the guild, and that it had been stolen from her workshop. It would be sold as far away from Mesomia as possible; and this dusty fair at the western tip of Jayangan was a long, long way from the Southern Marshlands of Mesomia.

Husam stared at it, this legendary carpet, in the midst of the grimiest stall at the far end of the bazaar, with one of the most villainous-looking stallholders in the whole of Jayangan, dressed in dirty robes and a filthy turban, smiling in an oily fashion at them both. 'Yes, yes, you come here,' he was saying. 'You look, sir, madam.'

Husam stared at it in disfavour. The carpet was garishly coloured and clumsily made. Badly drawn long-tailed, bright red birds with yellow eyes cavorted on a background of luminous green. Its fringe was ragged and its shape a little uncertain. 'What a disappointment!' the old man thought, sadly.

'Wonderful, isn't it?' said Kareen Amar, affectionately stroking it. 'I knew it at once.'

'Wonderful indeed,' smarmed the stallholder, 'and a good price for you, lovely lady, and your friend.' He put his head on one side, and smilingly named a price that made Husam's eyes nearly pop out of their sockets. The Jinn took no notice; she was too busy stroking the carpet, with a 'listening' look on her face, as if it were speaking to her.

'Ten thousand ruyiahs! You, sir, are a highway robber,' fumed Husam, with a glare at Kareen Amar's too-obvious preoccupation. 'It's just a cheap, ugly carpet. Worth one hundred ruyiahs at the most.'

The stallholder looked warily at the old executioner's tall, powerful form and strong face. 'Oh, no, sir,' he said, his ugly smile showing many teeth were missing, 'it's worth its weight in gold, and well your friend knows it. It's not the design or colours that are important, sir, it is what the carpet does. And where it's come from.'

'Flying carpets are lovely things,' said Husam, frowning. 'I've seen one or two. This one's ugly as your face, you old rogue. You are tricking us.'

'Sir!' said the stallholder, drawing himself up in mock outrage. 'Look at the lady; she knows it's the real thing.'

Kareen Amar was crooning to the carpet now; squatting on her heels, she had a faraway look on her face. She said quietly, 'It's ugly because the Enchantress is very young and hasn't yet learnt to create something that is beautiful as well as useful. But I can feel this carpet's spirit, and it's woven of fire, the best element of all.'

'And it has all kinds of modern features,' said the seller eagerly. 'Tell your lord, madam, that he should know how lucky he is to be allowed to purchase this unique piece.'

'Now look here —' began Husam angrily, but Kareen interrupted him gently.

'This is how it works. The carpet is imbued with firebird-spirit. This gives it the energy to fly long distances; it is the driving engine of the carpet.' She touched one of the birds, on its yellow eye, and muttered something under her breath. At once, the eye swivelled and lit up, almost like a tiny round computer screen. A map appeared on it, with dots moving around. 'This is the navigation system,' Kareen said, as proudly as if she had made it herself. 'Is it not very modern and new?' She touched another bird on its eye, and all at once there was a rustling sound, like a parachute opening, and suddenly, making them all jump, around the edges of the carpet leapt up a translucent, tall cover of some shimmering material, giving rather the effect of a pop-up caravan. Kareen grinned at the looks on their faces. 'This will protect us from the weather; it's woven from thread made by air-spiders, immensely strong and flexible. The beauty of this carpet is that you get both old and new, both spirit and human world represented here. It's perfect.' She touched the material and said a few words, and instantly it fell back again, melting away like dew on the grass.

'Like the lady said so perceptively,' said the stall-holder, quickly chiming in, 'it's perfect, and perfection needs to be paid for. I will not sell this marvel for less than – ten thousand ruyiahs.'

Husam spluttered, 'Keep your blinking carpet, you robber, you braying donkey, you ape's cousin!'

'A curse on your moustache!' said the stallholder, furious, his hand jumping to the short dagger at his side. 'You can't just insult a man like that, you –'

'Stop it,' said Kareen Amar quietly. She turned to look at the stallholder, full in the face, her eyes suddenly glowing very red. At the sight, he went pale, sweat stood out on his forehead, and he took a step back. 'You named a price to me when I first saw it, and that is what we will pay, no more, no less. Two thousand ruyiahs.' She reached into her pockets and drew out a wad of crumpled notes. 'Take it. The carpet is worth far more than that, but you are a thief. Count yourself lucky I do not send word to the workshops of the Marshlands that it is you who have stolen one of the new carpet prototypes. You know the fate the Marshlanders reserve for thieves and traitors.' The man stared fearfully at her as though he'd been turned to stone. Kareen Amar shoved the money into his unresisting hand. Then she got down on her knees and rolled the carpet up briskly. She put the bundle under her arm and looked crossly at Husam. 'What's the matter, goggling at me with great eyes? Time is pressing, my friend, and we have already spent too much time in this place. We must get down to the beach right away.' She turned her attention back to the stallholder. 'And if you breathe a word of this to anyone, grubby thief, be assured, on my honour as a free Desert-Jinn, that the Carpet Enchantresses of Mesomia will know where to find you.'

Leaving the terrified stallholder looking as if he wanted to disappear to the furthest ends of the earth, she stalked off, Husam following resignedly in her steps. 'Ah well,' he thought, 'if the carpet's driving element is fire, it should be all right. As Jinns are of that element, too, if the worst comes to the worst, Kareen Amar's own reserves will make the carpet stay up. Still, it's a wonder the carpet looks so clumsy and garish. Its creator must be a mere apprentice. God protect us, I'll have to bring my protective zummiyah water with me!'

'It can't fail,' said Kareen Amar over her shoulder, seemingly aware of what he was thinking. 'It was fated to be, that we would find this perfect thing. Besides, you know that the spirit Queen of the Southern Sea, Rorokidul, has promised to speed us on our way to Al Aksara. As she controls not only the waters but the sea winds, these have been directed to help us. From the beach at Kapalau, the winds will take us west over the ocean, skirting Alhind, then north to the lands of Al Aksara, up over the Gulf of Parsari and the Shining Sea, to land in the Ameeratan city of Jumana.'

'You seem to have been consulting your maps, Kareen,' said Husam dryly.

'I've thought of everything. All you have to do is bring your things, relax, and let me do the driving.'

'That's just the trouble. I'm not sure relaxing and letting you do the driving aren't mutually exclusive activities, Kareen Amar,' said Husam, laughing.

Four

The palace of the al-Farouks was bustling. Every-where he went, Khaled ran into servants running hither and thither, with paint pots, new carpets and furniture, and armfuls of ingredients for exotic dishes to tempt the palates of the eagerly awaited guests. Abdullah directed the operations. He seemed to have found some measure of relief from the worry of the fast-approaching deadline by throwing himself into all kinds of activity. Khaled kept out of the way, for he found it all rather unnerving. He wasn't sure of himself any more. Doubts filled his mind. How could a pair of strangers help in what was really a private family matter? Would they be in needless danger, these strangers on whom family burdens were to be placed? Why should any Jinn care about what might happen to him? Could ya do anything about fate, anyway? Every morning he woke up with dread in the pit of his stomach, thinking: 'It's one more day closer to my birthday.' He couldn't concentrate on anything.

His head full of fears and doubts, he wandered through the palace, escaping the crowds and activity. In one of the furthest wings he came to a deserted, cramped corridor, at the dark end of which was a little door. He opened the door and peered in. Beyond was a small room, crammed with boxes. Everything was covered in a fine film of dust. He couldn't remember having been here before. For something to do, for something to help him forget the questions that crowded into his head, he decided to investigate.

The doorway was low and he had to duck to go in. The ceiling was low, too, and he had to hunch his shoulders to walk about. The little room had an air of waiting, like a person holding their breath. There were no footprints on the floor, no handprints on the boxes. 'No-one has been in here for a very long time,' Khaled thought.

He went over to one of the boxes and opened it, sending a shower of dust to the floor. He peered in. The box was stacked with books. He picked one up. It had a mud-coloured jacket, with a title on it in gold: *Bricks and their Makers through the Centuries*. 'Well,' thought Khaled, 'that sounds like the dullest book you could ever read.' He opened the book; its pages crackled. 'No-one's ever opened it before,' he thought. He put it down and picked up another one.

A Short History of the Comma, it was entitled, in silver letters on green. 'But it isn't short at all,' thought Khaled, hefting the heavy thing in his hand. 'And it looks very boring indeed.' He looked at its first page. It had been presented to his grandfather, when he had been Ambassador of Ameerat to the Rummiyan Empire, far to the west. Khaled shook his head. 'Fancy writing such books, let alone reading them,' he murmured, aloud. 'Who on earth would waste their time?'

'You are an ill-mannered, ignorant child,' said a squeaky, thin voice. Khaled was so startled that he dropped both books on the floor. A cloud of dust rose from them.

'Can't you be more careful?' said the squeaky voice, peevishly. Khaled spun around to face the door. But there was no-one else in the room with him. It was quite empty. He was quite alone.

'Am I going mad?' he cried. 'I thought I heard –'

'I can't answer as to your mental state,' said the voice, even more sharply. Khaled stared as he caught sight of the thing hovering in the air just above him. It was a moth – or at least something that at first sight looked like a moth. It was about the size of one, and had a moth's wings, ragged and dark, and a moth's six legs, waving crankily at Khaled. But it was plain this was no ordinary moth: it had no insect features, but a humanish face with strange yellow, red-pupilled eyes and stiff, splendid whiskers. It had a segmented, dark brown and ochre furry body that was clad in what looked at first like oddly patterned cream silk but Khaled soon realised was actually paper covered with diagrams and figures.

'Well?' the moth-thing said in its thin voice. 'What's the matter? What are you staring at?'

'Forgive me,' stammered Khaled, at last, 'but I have never before seen –'

'Seen what? A Jinn as splendid as me?' The creature twirled its whiskers and looked mighty smug.

'Yes,' said Khaled, smiling inwardly. 'This must be one of the tribe of House-Jinns,' he thought. He had never met one before, though he'd seen them occasionally, just out of the corner of his eye, scurrying out of sight into shadows. House-Jinns didn't have anything like the power of wild Jinns – they were too tame, and too limited, especially one as tiny as this. 'You are of the Jinn?' he went on. 'I have never before imagined that Jinns could be as – as er . . . splendid as you,' he finished hastily, echoing the Jinn's own description of itself.

'Well, you've been badly taught,' said the Moth-Jinn, briskly. 'Know that I am Farasha, of the mighty, learned tribe of Yakabikaj, protectors of all books against bookworms, silverfish and decay. I have been assigned to protect such books as are in this room. My eldest brother, General Bikaj, and his platoons protect all the books your family has in the library. You will have seen the spell invoking our aid, of course; it is written above the doors of the library.'

There was indeed elegant scrolled writing above the library doors in the palace, but Khaled had never really paid attention to it. Now, though, he nodded, as Farasha went on, 'No-one has visited this room for a very long time. It has bothered me. But that is over. Now you have come here at last to pay homage to me, Farasha, the guardian Jinn of these books, as you should, and ask me questions.'

'Questions?' said Khaled. He looked at the little Jinn. Was it possible that —?

'Come on, then,' said Farasha, with splendid self-assurance, 'I give you permission to speak, and ask me what it is you wanted.'

'Er —' began Khaled uncertainly, then went on hurriedly, as Farasha's whiskers quivered and his eyes flashed, 'I was wondering, sir, if you might possibly be good enough to tell me whether, in your infinite wisdom and learned understanding, you have come across any information as to how curses can be unmade.'

Well, it was worth a try. He thought he might have overdone the flattery, but the Jinn didn't appear to find anything unusual in it.

'I do not think that it is possible to undo a curse,' said the Moth-Jinn. But its eyes were glittering with curiosity. 'Why do you want to know?'

Khaled sighed. 'Because there is a curse on the al-Farouks and if it is not unmade, I may die on my fifteenth birthday.'

'Dear me!' said Farasha, his eyes popping. 'What is said is said; what is done is done. You can no more change a curse than you can change a book once it is printed.'

'But you can issue a new edition,' said Khaled. 'You can find new information you didn't know when you first published the book, and publish again.'

'I have never heard of this. It cannot be true. None of my books has ever been published again,' said the Jinn firmly. ('I'm sure they weren't,' thought Khaled.) 'They were perfect to begin with. They cannot be improved or changed. That is the way of it. So it may well be with curses.'

The Jinn's words gave a strange kind of comfort to Khaled. If this pompous, naïve little creature in its piles of unread books thought that curses could not be lifted, then it was likely that they could. Even if it was difficult, or rare. It was likely the creature's brother, General Bikaj, would know more. But he'd have to go carefully, if he wanted to find out something from the library Jinn. Farasha had likely only talked to him because he was a lowly creature, curious, bored and lonely, protecting dusty unread tomes. Bikaj probably had a much more interesting life and no need for conversation with humans. It was likely, if conceit was a failing of the tribe, that his vanity would be overweening in any case. He would need an intermediary . . .

'Farasha, I wonder if I could ask a very great favour from you?'

'A favour?' squeaked Farasha rather eagerly. Then he pulled himself together, drawing himself up to his full – inconsiderable – height, as if remembering that he was a Jinn and should speak disdainfully to humans. 'What sort of favour? And if I grant it to you, I would expect something in return. I would expect you to restore these books to the place they should have – an honoured space on proper shelves, in a room which is visited.'

Khaled hesitated. His father had obviously not thought the dull books in here warranted any exposure at all – but then, there were many rooms in the palace he could arrange to have shelves put up in.

'I promise,' he said.

'I will hold you to that promise,' said the Jinn. 'Now, what is the favour you wanted to ask?'

'Will you please be kind enough to introduce me to your brother Bikaj? I am so impressed by your fine qualities and I would very much like to make the acquaintance of –'

That seemed to have been the wrong thing to say. The creature drew itself up. Its whiskers quivered indignantly, its ragged wings flapped. 'Impudent human! My brother is a great general, who commands great platoons. You do not ask to make his acquaintance, as if he could be your equal. You humbly beg to be allowed to come into his august presence!' His whiskers quivered with manufactured anger, but his eyes were full of eagerness and curiosity.

'As you wish,' said Khaled. 'I do beseech you, kind Farasha, to deign to beg leave of your august brother the General, Lord of the Library, that he might consent to bestow on me, his humble servant, the immense grace and favour of a few seconds in his company.'

'Hmm, better,' said the creature, 'though not quite long enough, and with not enough flourishes of rhetoric and syntax and graceful phrasing. For a son of the Shayk, you have a lot to learn. You should avail yourself of the opportunity right now to look at some of the books I protect, whose inimitable style will show you just what it is you are lacking. Why, even a fraction of —'

'Please, Farasha. Will you put my humble request in the best and most convoluted — I mean, gracious and beseeching — language, and convey it to your most marvellous brother, all-knowing Lord of the Library?'

'Do you promise that if I do so, I and my charges will be taken from this exile?'

'I do,' said Khaled fervently.

'Do you promise furthermore to have a spell of invocation to me, Farasha, of my choosing, written above the door of the room where we will be?'

'I promise,' said Khaled.

The Jinn hesitated, then suddenly burst out with, 'Do you promise that I can help you, too?'

Khaled smiled. 'Of course, Farasha. Just as you wish.'

'Very well,' said Farasha, and vanished, so rapidly and unexpectedly that Khaled was left blinking stupidly at the spot where the Jinn had been, for almost a full minute. When he'd recovered his senses, he shouted, 'Hey, wait, when will you do it? And when can I —'

But there was silence. Total, dusty silence.

Five

The flying carpet had proven to be a lot more comfortable than Husam had feared. Riding high and smooth in the clouds, they might as well have been sailing in a well-appointed cruise ship, insulated against the elements.

The worst moment had been when they took off – suddenly, jerkily, and straight up. Mind you, he would have felt the same gut-churning fear if it had been a plane. He liked it when his feet were firmly planted on the ground. It just wasn't natural for human beings to be flying high above the earth in any kind of contraption, no matter what gung-ho engineers or Jinns told you. He had closed his eyes and muttered several prayers under his breath, clicking at the prayer beads he held in one hand. When the carpet had finally straightened and smoothed out, he'd opened his eyes and seen, through the bubble of protection, a strange sight. Moving alongside them was a blurred, narrow grey face, half-visible through a white trail of vapour.

'Don't stare. It's a wind-spirit, and they can be rather proud,' hissed Kareen from her seat at the carpet's controls. 'It's a servant of Rorokidul's and will see us safely to our appointed path in the clouds, in a dimension midway between the human world and the spirit world.'

'Well away from plane flight paths, I hope,' said Husam a little faintly. 'I'd rather not see them hurtling past us.'

'Of course,' said Kareen. 'We will travel in a quiet passageway of time and space. No human being knows it.'

Time passed. All that could be seen through the bubble was thick white cloud which encased them as if in swathes of silk. Below them, the sea must be prowling, but Husam could neither hear it nor see it. No sound penetrated their strange vehicle. For a time, Husam slept, lulled by the almost complete isolation. When he woke, he saw Kareen was looking at him. She was grinning.

'We're nearly at Jumana, sleepy one,' she said. 'You see, it all went well. I know what I'm looking at, me, when I look at machines.'

As she spoke, the carpet suddenly lurched and jerked. 'What on earth —' shouted Husam, but he did not finish his sentence. The carpet plunged, so swiftly that it was like going down in a lift. White clouds flew past the bubble at an astonishing rate, then turned into hazy blue; and in less time than it takes to think it, the ground appeared beneath them, flying up towards them, or so it seemed. Husam fell over. He struggled to get up, but could not keep his balance.

Kareen Amar was hitting out at the carpet birds' eyes, their heads, their feet, but nothing was working. She was obviously in a panic. Flames shot out from her fingers; she was yelling something unintelligible. But still the carpet inexorably descended.

Suddenly, there was a jolt. The stench of burnt wool filled their nostrils. Kareen shrieked jumbled words. The carpet jerked, heaved, then all at once flopped. It rolled in on itself, sweeping Husam and Kareen towards the middle, tumbling over each other. It jerked again, heaved, then came down with an almighty thud that jarred Husam so hard it actually made his teeth rattle. The bubble of protection melted away, and they found themselves deposited in damp sand at the edge of the sea.

Kareen was the first to recover. She scrambled to her feet, hair on end, sparks flying off it, eyes glittering with rage. 'Stupid heap of rubbish!' she shrieked, striking out at the carpet with her foot. 'Stupid thief, stealing it before it was properly finished!'

Husam did not make the obvious retort. He was too shaken. 'The Light be praised, we are still alive,' he said, at last, and bending down, touched his forehead to the sand in thankfulness. Then he sat up, and looked around.

They had landed near a disused, barnacle-encrusted pier. In the distance could be seen wooden ships tied up at quays, and crowds of men unloading great bales of goods. They were in a variety of dress: loincloths and turbans and pants and headdresses, their weathered brown skin shining in the sun.

'This isn't Jumana,' said Husam rather glumly. 'But at least it's a port. Let's go and ask someone where we are.'

Kareen strode towards the quay, her wiry red hair bouncing with determined purpose on her shoulders, every stride showing a grim determination. 'If she had either the apprentice Enchantress, or the unfortunate thief under her hands at the moment, then woe betide them,' Husam thought, amused. Kareen Amar had lost face, the worst thing that could happen to a Jinn – even more so when it was her own fault.

'You want to know where you are?' said the bare-chested sailor they accosted. He grinned, showing the stumps of broken teeth, and pushed back the dirty red and white checked cloth that was wrapped around his head. 'Where did you land from? The moon?'

Husam gritted his teeth. 'My friend, where are we?'

'Shideh, of course,' said the other, after a long, hard look at Husam. 'Shideh, biggest port in Parsari, and biggest dump in the world.' Without another word, he turned his back on them and resumed unloading bags of charcoal, his muscles rippling under his sweating skin.

'Shideh!' said Husam and Kareen together.

'Well, I suppose it could be worse,' Husam went on. 'Jumana is directly across the gulf from Shideh. We can easily get there.'

'The carpet cannot fly; it will have to be repaired,' said Kareen sulkily. 'And I do not know how to do that.'

'Then we'll have to go by ship,' said Husam. 'But first, we must send a telegram to Abdullah al-Farouk, to tell him we will be late. He would doubtless send a boat over to meet us, but I think the sooner we get there, the better. We will arrange passage on the next ship.'

Six

When she'd arrived in the port of Shideh, Soheila had been utterly dismayed by its size. Great ocean-going dhows and sambuks rode high above the water, each one a different, lucky colour, with an all-seeing eye painted on its prow, to keep watch in the deep waters of the Shining Sea that led to Alhind. Smaller, lighter vessels, designed for the much shorter, much less dangerous trip across the Parsarian Gulf, flaunted a variety of coloured sails and sputtering engines; vast, rusty metal container ships, which carried goods from Rummiya and Radentengan and many other places beyond Dawtarn el 'Jisal, lay down one end of the harbour; and little tin boats making the journey up and down the Shideh River to the port, ducked and weaved amongst their great creaking, groaning cousins. And the noise! And the crowds! There were people from all the corners of the globe, it seemed to Soheila as she fought her way through the sweating press of sailors, labourers, porters, merchants and hawkers, trying to decide which ship's captain she should approach. If she'd had time and the heart to marvel, she could have spent hours looking at it all, at the human variety that flowed like a vast multicoloured sea over the wharves of the largest port in all of Parsari. But she had neither. All she could think about was getting as quickly as possible across the gulf.

She had thought she'd soon find a berth, but what she didn't know was that there was a great over-abundance of workers at the port of Shideh, and not enough work to go around. She went along the row of Jumana-bound boats, asking timidly if there was any work available. Most of the captains didn't even bother to answer; they glanced at her, saw a slight, skinny youth, and waved her away instantly. Those who did answer told her to get lost, couldn't the kid see they were busy, and they didn't take on scrawny rats in any case. Soheila could feel rage and panic mounting up in her like bile. She made wilder and wilder promises but nobody took any notice – they were too busy loading and unloading and gossiping at the tops of their voices. She was lost, in truth, in this vast crowd, and she had no idea of what to do.

For the first time, a sense of her own helplessness and ignorance overwhelmed her. Brought up in remote Sholeh, she had had no idea of what to expect in the big city. She had expected her determination would

just see her get what she wanted. She had not bar-
gained on not even being able to get across the water!

She was turning away from another fruitless
encounter with another indifferent, harassed sailor
when she saw an odd pair walking along the wharves:
a fiercely moustached, henna-bearded tall old man in
the black robes of a desert nomad, and a wild-looking
red-headed foreign woman with a sharp nose and
wearing an odd assortment of clothes. They were
carrying heavy bundles, and looked rather uncertain
as they gazed about them. The red-headed woman
wandered off to look at one of the ships. An idea
leapt into Soheila's mind. She dashed over to the
old man.

'Sir, are you looking for passage on a ship across the
gulf?'

The old man looked sharply at the young boy. 'Yes,
we are.' He spoke halting Parsarian, with a rather thick
accent. 'An Ameeratan accent,' thought Soheila,
delighted, 'or at least from one of the lands of Al
Aksara.'

'Sir, it is not easy to get passage, especially for
foreigners,' she said in a boy's voice. 'You need a middle-
man to negotiate these things.'

The old man raised his eyebrows and looked at the
thin boy. 'And you think you can do it?'

'Sir, I know I can. That is my job. That is what I
have been doing these many months,' Soheila lied,

fluently, grinning cheekily up at him, fully in her role as the street urchin Payem.

Husam smiled. 'I suppose everyone's got to live. What is your price then, boy, to help us negotiate?'

'Passage to Jumana with you.'

The old man looked at the boy sharply. 'Passage to Jumana? But I thought you were working here as –'

'Yes, but it does not pay much, sir. I need better work. I know there is a great deal of work over there, well-paying. And I want – I need to earn a lot more money than what I've been getting.'

'You are also very young,' said the old man, critically. 'Not more than twelve, I would think.'

'Thirteen, sir. Old enough to work, in my situation. I am an orphan. I came here from the mountains to try and find work. There is none here. My only hope is Jumana the White, where everyone can find a job.'

The old man nodded, his eyes softening. Soheila saw that she had touched him, and she was fiercely glad. Of course, she still had to negotiate a deal with some ship's captain, but that would be easy enough. Everyone knew ship's captains were grasping individuals. They did not care about helping the poor and desperate, but were happy enough to pocket money from more wealthy travellers.

'Very well,' said the old man, 'find us a ship, and a good deal. I will pay your passage.'

'Thank you, sir. You will not regret it.'

'What's your name, boy?'

'It is Payem.'

'Very well, Payem. We want to leave as quickly as possible, do you understand?'

'Yes, sir,' said Soheila. 'You will leave quickly.'

'Thank you, Payem.'

Soheila managed a small smile, and hurried off on her task. She made the sign of the Truthteller – two fingers against her chest – and breathed a prayer to Lord Akamenia, Flame of the World, to protect her. She touched the little silken sachet of ashes at her heart, and whispered, 'Soon, Zohreh, soon. The die is cast now.'

It didn't take long to find a suitable ship. The *Eagle* was a trim little dhow, painted blue, with a cargo of salt and cloth, a chugging, eager engine, and a cheerful captain named Hassan who seemed delighted to earn a little pocket money by taking on a few passengers. He bade Husam and Kareen welcome – and ignored Payem, for he was just a servant, after all – and rolled out a comfortable carpet for them to sit on. They were on their way.

Seven

The trip across the gulf was short and sweet, the sea glassy and smooth, and though Soheila's stomach churned a little at the unaccustomed motion, a real sense of excitement filled her. Within two hours, the great shimmering white towers, the golden sands, turquoise harbour and gleaming glass buildings of the fabled desert city of Jumana the White appeared on the horizon.

Never in her wildest dreams had she imagined anything quite as splendid as this city. Jumana the White was the richest city in all of the oil-rich kingdoms of Al Aksara, not only because of the black gold that had transformed the modest port into a great metropolis in the last fifty years, but because of its ancient trading networks. Indeed, it was fair to say Jumana was the richest city in all the lands of el 'Jisal. That much she knew from books. It's one thing to read about something in a book, however, and quite another to see it. In its shimmering white beauty and glittering grandeur, it looked like an enchanted place, like something conjured by the powerful Jinn of the Lamp, in the old story of Aladdin. As the dhow glided towards its anchorage point on the harbour wall, the urchin Payem just kept staring, as if spellbound by the sight.

But Kareen and Husam, not at all impressed – after all, both of them knew Jumana of old – bustled around getting all their bags together. During the voyage, Kareen Amar had managed to wash the carpet and dry it in the sun, and it was now safely rolled up in a hessian bag sold to them by kind Captain Hassan. Its workings would have to be fixed, but it should not be too difficult to find flying carpet doctors and mechanics in Jumana – the place attracted great craftsmen from everywhere, and there were many Mesomian refugees here.

The wooden gangplank clattered onto the quay. Captain Hassan farewelled them, shook their hands, and accepted their thanks – and Husam's extra banknote with a twinkling, but dignified, pleasure. 'Good luck, and may the Light bless you, my friends,' he said. 'I think you will have a wonderful time in Jumana. It is one of the wonders of the world.' He looked at Payem, bringing up the rear. 'And you, boy – here, all your dreams can come true. You can go from rags to riches in a year, it is said, if you work hard enough. Perhaps next time I see you, you will have rings on your fingers and a fine suit on your back, and you will own a fleet of ships?' He laughed uproariously, slapped Payem, not unkindly, on the back, and turned back to ordering his crew to unload.

The quay was wide, very white and scrubbed, and the street that ran beside it was lined with large, graceful palm trees and bright shrubs. When you saw such lushness it was hard to remember Jumana was built directly on the desert sands, and that all its water was purified sea water. But they didn't have much time to think about it, for just then a car drew up before them, in a rush and hiss of tyres. It was a big, gleaming black car, with a carving of a golden eagle prominent on its hood, like a figurehead on the prow of a ship. A tall, uniformed chauffeur got out. He was dressed in black and gold livery, with a golden eagle emblazoned on the left side of his chest. On his head was a snowy white cloth, with a thick black silk cord holding it in place, and on his hip, discreetly but unmistakeably, was a gun in a black leather holster. He looked impressive, but also rather like a character in a film, and his words did nothing to dispel that impression.

'Good afternoon to our honoured guests. I am Omar al-Sayara, personal driver to Lord Abdullah al-Farouk,' he said in a deep, resonant voice. 'You are most welcome to Jumana.' His face showed no reaction to the rather motley sight they presented; obviously, he'd been well briefed. 'My master sends his apologies for not coming to meet you himself; he only just received your telegram. Please, sirs and ladies, step this way.' He opened the car door with a flourish, and stood back to usher them in.

Kareen Amar went in first. Just before Husam got into the car, out of the corner of his eye he saw Payem hovering, with a naked look of wistful longing on his face. An impulse of pity made him say to the driver, 'Friend Omar, is there any work at your master's palace?'

Omar controlled his expression with an obvious effort. 'Work, sir?'

'Don't worry, Omar,' said Husam with a little chuckle, 'it's not for me – it's for that ragamuffin over there. He helped us get our passage on the *Eagle*. And he's come to Jumana looking for work.'

'I happen to know the second cook is urgently looking for a kitchen boy,' Omar allowed, with a glance at the boy. 'What is the boy's name? And where is he from?'

'Payem,' said Husam. 'He's from Parsari, but I think he might have Ameeratan blood too – he speaks the language quite well, if with an accent.' He beckoned to Payem. 'You didn't have any particular work in mind, friend, when you said you wanted to obtain employment here?'

A timid hope flared in the child's face. He scuffed a battered shoe at the ground. 'No, sir. I'm prepared to do anything.'

'Well, this man says there's a kitchen boy urgently wanted, in the palace of the al-Farouks.'

'Oh, sir!' said the boy, his thin face flushing, his pleading eyes on the imperturbable Omar. 'I have done much of this kind of work, for my family. I would work very hard indeed, if you should give me this chance.'

'It is not for me to give you the chance,' said Omar, 'but for the second cook. However, I am of the mind she will be grateful if you came.' He looked down his aquiline nose at the boy. 'Take the bus at the Gold Market stop,' he went on, not unkindly, motioning to a bus stop in the distance, 'and ask the driver for the al-Farouk corner. Everyone knows it. Go around to the back gate and ring the bell. Tell the gatekeeper I, Omar al-Sayara, sent you, and tell them you have come for the kitchen boy post.'

'Oh, thank you so much, sir,' said Payem, humbly bending his head. Husam saw he still looked uncertain.

'I'll warrant you don't have any fare for the bus, is that right?'

Payem nodded. Husam pulled some coins out of his robe pocket and gave them to Payem. The boy flushed again, to the roots of his hair.

'Thank you, sir,' he murmured. 'You are very kind.'

'Nonsense,' said Husam, 'just realistic. Good luck, friend. And take care.'

But he spoke to thin air. Payem was already haring

off down the street, as fast as his skinny legs could carry him.

'What were you doing,' hissed Kareen to Husam, when he got into the car, 'passing the time of day with that little thief?'

'He's no thief,' said Husam crossly, 'just a poor boy who needs a job.'

'Hmm,' said Kareen, her eyes narrowing, 'there's something about that boy I don't like at all, something sly and devious. You should have let him be.'

Husam shrugged, unwilling to argue with the Jinn. She often got strange ideas in her head, and she had no notion of human pity. That was the way she was made, it couldn't be helped. In any case, he'd done what he could for the boy. It was up to him now.

Soheila fought her way on to a crowded bus. As it jerked away from the stop, she thanked Akamenia under her breath for having looked after her so well. She was actually on her way to a job at her enemy's house. Truly, the Lord Akamemia was great!

As the bus rattled through the streets, though, her sense of exultation gave way to a growing sense of mixed awe and resentment. This city was so wealthy, so fortunate, so clean and shining. Though there was a lot of traffic, the size and sweep of the great broad streets meant it flowed well. She pressed her nose against the window, taking in all the sights they were passing: the

Gold Market, under its vast, burnished blue and gold cupola of a roof; the gleaming white and clear glass towers that were homes to banks and businesses dealing in oil and gold and diamonds; the Cloth Markets, where silks and brocades and linens and wools of the finest quality shimmered in great streaming shining rivers from wooden stalls; the enormous Carpet Bazaar; the golden roofs and slender white towers of the many beautiful houses of worship; the vast shopping complexes of white stone and green glass; and the large white and pale pink and blue and yellow mansions lining the road.

The streets were full of people enjoying the cool early-evening air. There were tall Ameeratan men in snowy-white robes and elegantly placed and folded headcloths, black or gold silk cords holding the cloth down; many of them were talking on tiny, jewel-like mobile phones that flashed in the sun. There were flocks of black-clad, gauze-veiled Ameeratan women, elegant high-heeled shoes protruding from under the hems of their sober long coats as they walked. There were flurries of little girls in colourful dresses, and little boys in noisy gangs. There were proud desert women, peering fiercely from behind gilded leather masks that made them look for all the world like hooded falcons; and tall black men and women from Aswadd with heavy gold jewellery around their necks. There were swaggering warlords from the far, wild tribal areas in the high mountains many weeks' journey to the north-west, in clothes of savage elegance: woollen tunics and pants, black fur-trimmed cloaks, and powder-blue turbans. One or two of them even had the skin of wild beasts flung over their shoulders, the heads still grinning in death. There were haughty Parsarian noblemen; and tourists from the Rummiyan Empire, in light clothes and enormous hats, faces red from the sun, astonished eyes peering everywhere. There were stern-faced Pumujisal preachers in pure white robes and black cloaks; and traders from Faraona and Masrikhan in sharp suits and even sharper haircuts.

But Soheila saw that there weren't only the rich, the leisured and the comfortable here on display in the streets of Jumana: there were also crowds of henna-bearded men from the dirt-poor villages of Alhind, pushing carts, sweeping streets, tending gardens, working on roads, and unloading ships and vans. There were young girls in crisp maids' uniforms, who from their features looked like they were from Jayangan, or the islands around it, hurrying on errands; and Mesomian refugees and other poor exiles from the four corners of the Mujisal world, trying to eke out a living by selling cheap watches, mobile phones and sunglasses from trays slung around their necks.

Soheila shivered a little, remembering where she was bound. She was to be a lowly servant in the house of her family's enemies. How would they treat her, the descendants of wicked Kassim? What was she doing, putting her head into the lion's –

'Al-Farouk corner!' yelled the driver, as the bus swung into a quiet street. 'Al-Farouk corner!' Her heart thumping in her chest, Soheila jumped up. This was it. Now she could not even think of turning back.

Eight

They were here at last! Khaled felt his heart beating fast with nervousness as the great doors opened, and the head footman announced the arrival of their guests. Though he thought Husam was a fine figure of a man, Khaled was taken aback by Kareen Amar's appearance, not having imagined that a Jinn might look like a mad Rummiyan wanderer, of the kind you occasionally saw in the street. Abdullah limped towards them with hand outstretched, and welcomed them in the fullest possible manner, with every elaboration of Ameeratan courtesy and politeness. Khaled nervously waited for his father to finish the preliminary politenesses so he could be introduced in his turn.

He jumped as a voice spoke in his ear. 'Bikaj will see you now.'

Farasha! What a time to choose. 'It's not possible,' Khaled mouthed. 'Not right now.'

'What do you mean, not right now?' The little creature's wing was tickling his ear, just under the folds of his headcloth. Khaled gave an involuntary shudder. 'We have guests, Farasha,' he whispered.

'I can see that. Who are they?'

'My father's friend, Husam. And the other is a Jinn, a Desert-Jinn.'

'Well!' said Farasha, giving an excited hop. 'We have not had one of those in the house for a long time.' Then he seemed to remember what he'd come for. 'But you must come. Brother Bikaj wants to see you now.'

'I can't, Farasha,' whispered Khaled, desperately.

'Oh, but you must. I moved heaven and earth to prevail upon Bikaj to talk to you. He doesn't like to talk to humans, normally.'

'I can't!' yelled Khaled, goaded beyond endurance. Now everyone was staring at him. He went bright red and mumbled, 'I'm sorry – forgive me – a moth crawling along the back of my neck –'

His father was looking at him in astonished dismay. He said sharply, 'Khaled, you forget yourself. Kindly remember who and where you are.'

'Forgive me,' said Khaled miserably. He felt cautiously at his ear. Farasha was gone. Khaled went through all the customary courtesies with a strong sense that he had really blown it. The guests would think he was a rude fool; and he had missed his opportunity with Bikaj. Nothing was going right.

Refreshments were brought, and then the doors were shut, and Abdullah turned to his son. 'I've already written to Husam and Kareen to tell them everything I know about the curse,' he said, 'but now you can explain what you have worked out yourself.' Khaled began to tell them about the various books he'd read, and the insights that had come to him. Husam and Kareen listened without interrupting. When Khaled had finished, they looked at each other and Husam said, 'It's not going to be easy to break the curse, is it, Kareen?'

'No,' said the red-headed Jinn.

'But it's possible?' said Abdullah anxiously.

'It might be. It just might be,' said Kareen.

'And what of Khaled's notion that he is in extra danger because this is the hundredth anniversary?'

Kareen glanced at Khaled. 'He is right,' she said.

'But the last thing you must do is give in to fear,' said Husam gently. 'We are here, and we will do all we can to protect you.'

Kareen looked at Khaled. 'Nothing will happen till the appointed day,' she said, 'but you must still be careful. And trust in Husam. He has faced more unearthly things than any other man I know. Now then, if you will excuse me, I will start my investigations at once, among the House-Jinn. They are foolish and limited creatures, no match at all for a powerful magician such as Zohreh must have been, but they might know one or two useful titbits.'

And with that she was gone. Husam turned to Khaled. 'Don't worry. We still have time. And in that time, we will find out a great deal.'

'I am sure we will,' said Khaled, gulping, trying to sound brave and unruffled and sure. He was glad to see his father looked much happier. But as for him, the doubts had not quite disappeared. He couldn't help thinking that with each moment that passed he got closer and closer to what Kareen had called the 'appointed day'.

A little later, he asked to be excused in his turn. Deep in rather gloomy thought, he wandered outside, down the path that led to the rose garden. He sat for a while, inhaling the fragrance of the beautiful flowers that made him think of his mother. His father said this had been her favourite spot. Tears pricked at his eyes. 'Well,' he thought, 'if it is all useless, if in a few days I will die, at least I have the consolation that I might see Mother again, in the lands beyond death.'

'Sir,' said a small voice, 'excuse me, sir, but I was told to go to the kitchens, through the garden. I seem to have lost my way.'

Khaled started. He saw a very thin, rather ragged youth, with burning, enormous blue eyes, standing humbly some distance away. Their eyes met. A strange shiver came over Khaled, though for the life of him he didn't know why. Turning his eyes away, he said hastily,

'You will need to go down this path, turn right into the almond grove, and then left into the orange orchard. There you will see the herb garden, and directly in front of you, set in the wall, the back door to the kitchens.'

'Thank you, sir,' said the boy, turning to leave.

'Stop,' said Khaled impulsively, 'you're new here, aren't you? I haven't seen you around before. What's your name?'

A strange expression leapt into the boy's eyes. 'I'm – I'm Payem –' he stammered. 'I'm – I'm going to work in the kitchens. Omar al-Sayara said –' Khaled saw that the boy looked fearful – of him – and he felt ashamed. He hadn't meant to bully the child. 'Of course,' he said, 'forgive me, I didn't mean to –'

But the boy had gone, scampering along the way Khaled had indicated to him.

Soheila could hardly believe she was actually in the place where it had all begun. As she raced through the massive gardens of the al-Farouks she hardly saw anything of the beauty around her. She was now on enemy territory and it would take all her guile and courage to honourably fulfil the task she'd set herself. Was the spirit of her ancestor still here, in this place where she had been so foully slain? If it was, that spirit would be looking to see whether her descendant was worthy of being her avenger.

She didn't think twice about the boy in the rose garden. No doubt he was a member of the household – and that meant he was someone she couldn't look at as she'd look at another human being, or her heart might fail her. She did not dare to think on the kindness she'd encountered so far, from Omar to the gatekeeper to the boy in the rose garden; she was here to carry out revenge. The easy way in which she'd found herself in the heart of enemy territory must mean that her mission was blessed by Lord Akamenia himself, and therefore holy.

She reached the herb garden and ran through it to the kitchen door. She creaked it open, and was immediately in the noisy backways of a very busy kitchen. Timidly posing a few questions, she was soon directed to the second cook, a very tall, rather large and majestic black Nashranee woman from Aswadd called Miss Josephine. She had shrewd, cross eyes and was dressed in a rather magnificent shade of crimson, her closely plaited red-hennaed hair lying against the sides of her round black head like the carvings on a statue, and a golden Nashranee heart symbol swinging on a golden chain around her thick neck. When Soheila meekly told Miss Josephine that her name was Payem, and that Omar had sent her to fill the position of kitchen boy, the Aswaddi boomed, 'Very well, you can start at once. Over there – the chief spice-maker needs some more ground coriander, at the double. What are you staring

for, boy? Get over there at once!' She fetched the boy
a cuff across the ear that sent him sprawling, and
turned back to her main work of harassing the under-
cooks. Soheila picked herself up and scuttled across to
where Miss Josephine had pointed.

The chief spice-maker turned out to be a deaf
mute called Rajiv – a thin, almost skeletal, Alhindi man
with a sunken chest under his stained white tunic. He
deftly made himself understood with a variety of
expressive gestures, and his eyes were kind. He showed
Soheila what he wanted, and she was soon kept busy
grinding and mashing and mixing.

It was an extraordinary place, this kitchen. It was
as big as a normal family house – or probably even
bigger. Certainly it was much bigger than Soheila's
own house back in Sholeh. It was full of rushing
people. The sight of all the food, the extravagance of
the dishes, the effortless wealth that all this represented,
tightened her heart – and her resolve – even more. She
would be patient; she would learn as much as she could
about the al-Farouks so she would know how best to
strike, and when, and whom.

Kareen prowled around the corridors of the palace like
a red-headed ghost, startling servants who came unexpectedly across her, and who assumed that she was
some kind of mad Rummiyan that their master, for
inscrutable reasons of his own, had allowed to stay in

the train of his other guests. Kareen didn't care what anyone thought; she was intent on following the trails of the other Jinns who lived in this place. It would take a while to become familiar with them, she knew. House-Jinns – with their settled, clannish ways – would be very suspicious of a wandering spirit, being not sure where to place her in caste and hierarchy, especially given that she had wandered so far from her native habitation. It would take patience and diplomacy to work out the correct ways to approach them – and Kareen had neither quality in significant quantities. She was independent, dismissive of niceties, and determined to do it her own way.

She had known there was some kind of House-Jinn hanging around Khaled back in the grand salon, causing the youth's strange behaviour. If she'd had a tiny bit more time she would have called it out but it had disappeared before she'd had a chance to do so. She had caught its name, Farasha, on the lips of the boy, but not where it came from or what part of the caste it operated in, and that was the important thing with House-Jinns, especially in a palace like this one. The upper-class ones were so haughty they wouldn't even look at you; the middle-class ones were so determined to be upper-class that they treated you with scorn; the lower-class ones liked to get their own back on the others, and so might lie, out of pure mischief. Still, it was the lower-class ones Kareen found it easier to speak to, especially now that, after her long habitation in Jayangan, she had become a trifle rusty on the whole protocol of Al Aksara House-Jinn tribes.

She had prowled along so far that she had reached the end of the family's and the guests' quarters. She was in the servants' quarters now. This was more like it, she thought, sniffing determinedly along the corridors, looking into every room. This was where she'd find her allies, her go-betweens.

She pushed open a door and found herself in the bathroom. It was not like the guest bathrooms, of course, but it was clean and cool, the concrete floors scrupulously scrubbed, as were the plain white baths, showers, lavatories and other fittings. Kareen held her breath. She could feel a friendly, approachable presence here. She waited, listened, then bowed in every direction and said, 'Compatriot of the Fire, kinsman of the Secret People, honoured friend, I, Kareen Amar, salute you, and beg leave to speak with you.'

'You have a funny accent, friend,' said a cheerful, roguish voice, 'and you're one of those wanderers, aren't you?' The Jinn had manifested himself as a kind of shadow on the glass of one of the shower screens; only his yellow, sparkling eyes could have been clearly seen, and only for a second, by any human who might have wandered in. But Kareen Amar, with the sensitivity of her kind, could see his real fire-shape.

'I am Kareen Amar,' she said with great dignity,

'wandering songstress of the Jinn, and my accent is strange to you because I have dwelt long in Jayangan and other places far to the east, gathering music. What may be your name, honoured compatriot?'

'My name is Hamarajol,' said the Jinn, 'and this is my place, this place of splashes and smells.' He gurgled with laughter. 'The other Jinns look down on me because of it, but that is no concern of mine. Welcome, wandering songstress, who is the first in hundreds of years to call me "honoured". What may I do for you?'

'I need some information on the clans in this house, please, honoured Hamarajol,' said Kareen Amar.

'Ah, that will be a pleasure, but it will take time,' said the Jinn. 'There are so many great ones in this house, my friend – so many who consider themselves great, that is. Where do you want me to start?'

'With Farasha,' said Kareen Amar. Hamarajol gave a low whistle. 'Farasha? He's hardly great or important, only a rung above me, really, though you wouldn't think it, the way he preens himself.'

'Never mind, he may be of use,' said Kareen Amar. And quickly, she told Hamarajol a little about what they were there for, and what she'd seen in the grand salon. The other Jinn gave a gurgling laugh again. 'Well, flush me down!' he exclaimed coarsely. 'They don't half want to perform miracles, those Clay People.'

'Don't they always,' said Kareen.

'Now then, our friend Farasha,' said Hamarajol, 'is

the Jinn of neglected books. His home is not very far from here. Come with me, we will speak to him together.'

Nine

Abdullah had spared no expense for the welcoming dinner that evening. The long, polished table in the main dining room was set with an ancient, delicate lace tablecloth from Wardah, the Rose City of Masrikhan, heavy, carved solid silver cutlery from Alhind, and gold and crystal goblets from Leonica, a famous canal city in the Rummiyan Empire, while an amazing butter sculpture of the al-Farouk family symbol, the golden eagle, was the table centrepiece. Ferns and roses and sprays of blossom, airfreighted from distant cities, filled the room with scent and colour, and the waiting staff were dressed in black and gold livery.

If the setting was magnificent, the food was even more so, for the cooks had excelled themselves. There were dishes of the best Parsarian caviar, with fresh bread and lemon slices; platters of fragrant rice, sprinkled with powder of gold; steaming lamb stews, and chicken with plump apricots, and juicy meat skewers, and whole fish with a glazing of herbs and spices; beautiful green and red salads, and eggs stuffed with spinach and nuts; and honey pastries, light apricot sherbets and fragrant rosewater sweets.

While Husam ate heartily, and Abdullah chatted companionably with him, Kareen was not even at the table, for Jinns rarely eat. Khaled could hardly keep still, and only toyed with his food. He wondered what Kareen was doing. He wondered when Farasha would come back. He wondered if even now, Zohreh's ghostly presence was gathering in the shadows, ready to strike a last, devastating blow. He wondered if there was any point to anything at all ...

In the kitchen, Soheila had no time to ponder or wonder. She was on her feet all night, running from one end of the kitchen to the other, fetching, carrying and doing all kinds of odd jobs for all kinds of people. She was not the only kitchen boy. There were two others, including a rather cheerful Mesomian refugee boy, Ismail, who took the newcomer under his wing. It was soon apparent that a kitchen boy's work was never done, and that as he was on the bottom of the entire pecking order in the kitchen, anyone and everyone could demand things of him, be it crushing spices, or sweeping, or fetching things from the larders, or washing platters, or chopping onions, or throwing out rubbish.

Fortunately, there was the odd break now and again. Despite her brisk manner and tough regime,

Miss Josephine was at heart fair and kindly. She knew her workers needed a rest and a drink every few hours or so. Soheila was able then to catch her breath and her wits, wipe the sweat from her brow, and guzzle down a glass of cold sweet mint tea, which soothed her poor parched throat. She answered Ismail's questions, inventing for Payem a penniless widowed mother in Shideh who had many children to support and needed all the money he could send home. As Ismail hailed from Mesomia, it made no difference what she told him; he'd never been to Parsari and likely never would, especially since the two countries were still technically at war with each other. But he was eager to tell her all about his own family, who'd had to flee The Vampire's cruel rule and now lived all piled in together in a tiny flat in one of the poorer suburbs of Jumana; he was very pleased that his wages were helping to send his younger sisters to school. Wages were good here, he said, especially in the al-Farouk household, where though you were expected to work hard, you were treated well, looked after if you got sick, and given bonuses on holy days and festivals. It wasn't the case everywhere in Jumana, he said; some of his friends had to suffer under cruel or indifferent masters. Soheila listened with only half an ear. She had no intention of getting caught up in someone else's life, and she didn't want to hear good things about the al-Farouks.

At last, well past midnight, the two kitchen boys were told they should go to bed and get some rest before the work for breakfast started. Ismail took Payem into the dormitory for the younger male servants, and showed him a trundle bed that would be his, and the communal bathroom down the hall. Fortunately for Soheila, there was one closed cubicle containing a shower and a toilet, and this she was able to use in privacy, and then change into clean, if patched, pyjamas. Lying down on the surprisingly comfortable bed, the urchin from Parsari had a sudden, dispiriting image of her shabby home.

A hundred years ago, the Melkior clan had been on a level similar to the al-Farouks. Zohreh the Akamenian had been as rich and well connected as Kassim al-Farouk, her family no doubt much more ancient and noble. Now her descendant slaved as a lowly kitchen boy in the servants' quarters of the al-Farouk palace, while Kassim's own descendants were as ridiculously, overwhelmingly rich as the Prince of Ameerat himself, not far behind the Emperor of Parsari, who had once reigned in that country. Ismail had said the Shayk received kings, ambassadors, presidents and great men and women from all over the world in this palace. The family rode and hunted with the Prince of Ameerat and the fierce king of neighbouring Riyaldaw, in whose vast, troubled desert kingdom was situated the supreme holy shrine of the Mujisals, the House of Light, where the Heaven Stone reposed as token of God's protection of all Mujisals. The al-Farouks were, so Ismail said, the second-greatest family in Ameerat, and amongst the ten great families of the whole of the holy peninsula of Al Aksara itself. He said this in tones of great admiration and wonder, but Soheila's heart twisted with hatred at these words. It was so unfair and so unjust, and it couldn't be allowed to stand. She placed Zohreh's ashes under her pillow for safety. 'I promise, Grandmother of Grandmothers, I promise to avenge you, and make these arrogant people taste the bread of bitterness.'

It seemed that there was a presence in the room with her, something that she could not yet see or hear. Her heart constricted with excitement, and a touch of fear, for instinctively she knew who it was. 'Grandmother Zohreh,' she whispered, and fell asleep on the name. In her dreams, she saw again the hooded figure she had seen back home, the one who had beckoned her to come to this place. And now, the figure beckoned her into the very heart of the palace itself.

Kareen slipped into Husam's room late into the marches of the night and told him what she had learnt from Farasha. The Moth-Jinn had promised he'd get Kareen and her friends an audience with his esteemed brother tomorrow afternoon. Furthermore, he'd talked at length about the way in which the House-Jinns operated. Kareen had played on his highly developed snobbery to get the information, encouraging him by calling him 'Oh Great Historian of the House-Jinns', and 'Oh Fount of Great Learning' and other such epithets, so that Farasha had visibly swelled with pride and had not even made any demands in return for the favours he was being asked.

'He is a foolish, vain, shallow creature,' summed up Kareen, 'but a useful one. And curious, too, which is unusual and rather reprehensible in a Jinn, but helpful for us.'

'If he could only hear you . . .' said Husam, smiling.

Kareen frowned a little. 'I made quite sure he couldn't,' she said stiffly. 'He has very small powers only, easily overthrown by mine. I do not know what Brother Bikaj will be like, but I have yet to meet a Book-Jinn that I can truly like. They are the most conceited and arrogantly complacent of all House-Jinns. They think all Musician-Jinns are empty-headed creatures, vastly inferior to literary ones, and they perorate endlessly and tiresomely on all subjects under the sun, including ones about which they are completely ignorant, like music.'

'Oh dear, Kareen,' said Husam, laughing, 'we might be in for an entertaining time with Brother Bikaj and little Farasha, judging from those ruffled feathers of yours.'

'Hmm,' said Kareen, 'they'd better not annoy me too much, those House-Jinns. Anyway, here's another thing Farasha told me: there is a Mesomian trader in the Carpet Bazaar who will be able to help us repair our flying carpet. Farasha knows this because his realm, the repository for boring books, is also the place where they store packing boxes. One of the great events of his dull life occurred a few months ago, when a new box was brought into the storeroom. It had come from this trader's shop and Farasha had a short conversation with a stray carpet worm who crawled out from it. I tell you: the creature looks down on me because he's a Book-Jinn, but he lives so tediously that a new box coming into his realm is an event, and he has *conversations* with such lowly things as carpet worms!'

'Shocking indeed,' agreed Husam, hiding a smile under his thick moustache. 'But it sounds good, anyway. Let's go there tomorrow morning, eh?'

'Very well,' said Kareen, and so saying, she stumped out of the room back to her own quarters, where she didn't sleep at all, for Jinns have no need of sleep, but instead weaved together a new song, to remember her arrival back in the land of her origins. And if any human in the sleeping palace heard that song, late, very late, it disturbed nobody, for it was a lovely, sweet song with a haunting melody, that appeared to come to them in a dream. But the House-Jinns heard it clearly, and they knew that one of the old Jinns, the free Jinns, the wandering desert spirits, was at loose in their calm and ordered place, and that anything, but anything, might happen now.

Ten

Khaled woke very early, his mouth dry, his eyes gritty. He had not slept well at all, and his dreams had been full of images of fire and blood. He sat up in bed and looked at the clock. It was only five am. And only three days till his birthday.

He jumped up, got dressed and slipped quietly out of his room. Nobody was about in this part of the house, and nobody saw him as he headed along the corridors to the library.

It was a lovely, cosy room, lined with enormous mahogany bookshelves, some open, some glass-fronted. Large winged armchairs and low tables occupied the centre of the room, and at the sides were stacked a couple of stepladders, to reach books that were higher up. There were ancient silk carpets on the floor, a little worn in places, but magnificent. A tall old mirror, beautifully carved, stood in one corner.

It was dim in the library, and very quiet. Khaled

opened a curtain a little so he could see. Some grey light inched in. He stood nervously in the centre of the room. 'Lord Bikaj,' he whispered, 'please, I ask you, come to my aid.'

Silence. He repeated the phrase, rather hopelessly this time. When there was still no answer, he said out loud the words of the formula written above the door that invoked the protection of Book-Jinns. But still there was nothing.

It was then that he heard the hurrying footsteps, coming straight for the door. Khaled didn't stop to think; he dived down behind one of the armchairs.

The doors opened. It was not a man's tread, not a Jinn's glide, but light, hesitant. A child's footsteps? Khaled was puzzled. He heard the creak of one of the glass-fronted bookcase doors opening. Very quietly, he peered round the side of the chair.

There was a thin, shabby figure standing in front of the bookcase, reaching out for a book on the topmost shelf. Khaled made a slight movement of surprise, and the figure heard it. It whirled around and dropped the book – revealing the intruder to be not a clerk, as Khaled expected, but Payem, the new Parsarian kitchen boy he'd seen in the garden the day before.

Payem's huge blue eyes were fixed on Khaled. There was a depth of emotion in them that Khaled took to be fear. He started towards the boy. 'Don't be scared,' he said gently. 'There's nothing to be afraid of.'

The boy looked like he wanted to flee, but somehow he held his ground. Faintly, he whispered, 'Sir, forgive me, I didn't mean to –'

'You haven't done anything wrong, that I know of,' said Khaled. He picked up the book the boy had dropped and looked at it. '*Legends of the Akamenians*,' he read. It was one of the books he himself had consulted during his investigations, though he'd had a hard job of it, knowing only a little Parsarian as he did. 'It's in your language,' he went on. 'You are interested in the fire-people, Payem? Or are you one?'

The blue eyes stared at him, the fear now quite naked in them. Khaled remembered that in Parsari, fanatics prowled around looking for Akamenians to beat up or even kill. He said, 'It's all right. You don't need to worry, even if you are an Akamenian, Payem. No-one is forced to renounce their faith in this house, as long as they don't try to convert others.'

Payem swallowed and tried to speak, but could not. Khaled held out the book. 'Take it with you, if you like. It's something to read at night. And maybe you can tell me a bit more about it. I wasn't able to read a lot of it. I don't know your language well enough.'

'Sir,' said Payem, breathlessly, 'I cannot take it, the other servants, they'll – they won't understand. I am sorry, forgive me for coming into this place without permission, I understand I'll be punished, but – I love reading, and I . . .'

'Don't be silly,' said Khaled crossly. 'Why would you be punished, just for wanting to read? We aren't like that, in this family. I will ask my father if you can come in here regularly to read, if you'd like –'

Something flashed in Payem's eyes. He looked like he was about to say something, when suddenly they heard Husam's booming voice, followed by Kareen's rapid tones. Payem shot a pleading glance at Khaled, then in a swift movement whipped behind one of the heavy velvet curtains and was instantly gone from sight behind the deep folds. Not an instant too soon, for the doors opened with a crash, and Husam and Kareen walked in.

'Well, look who's here so bright and early!' said Husam, cheerfully. 'You a bookworm like your father, young Khaled?'

'Well, sir,' said Khaled, 'I do like to read, but I'm not sure I read quite as much as my father.' He was intensely aware of Payem hidden behind the curtains.

Husam looked around him. 'You know, Khaled, when I was young, I came into this place with Abdullah only once. I wasn't a reader back then, but I remember it impressing me a great deal, even so. Of course, Abdullah must have added greatly to this library since then.'

Kareen Amar was not paying any attention to them. She was prowling around the room. Her gaze was not at the bookshelves but at something invisible, beyond their ken; her face had that listening look again. She said, startling them, 'General Lord Bikaj of the Yakabikaj, Protector of all Books in this Library, I, Kareen Amar, Compatriot of Fire, bring you fair greetings!'

She inclined her head, and waited. All was deathly still in the library. Khaled held his breath. Would the recalcitrant Library-Jinn make an appearance now?

Kareen Amar repeated her greetings, the beginning of a tiny frown appearing on her face as she spoke. Again, she inclined her head. Again, there was deathly silence. A third time she repeated it, her voice noticeably more impatient; then suddenly, came a high, petulant voice.

'Kareen Amar, I hear you. What do you want?'

'Audience with you, General Bikaj,' she said.

'So I hear from Farasha. Why does a wandering spirit come into the settled places? Why does a daughter of the desert serve humans?'

'We all serve humans,' said Kareen, 'except for those who followed Iblis, as you know, General Bikaj.'

'You must not say that accursed one's name!' screeched the petulant voice. 'It is forbidden, in this realm of mine.'

'Yet it is there even in the holy books,' said Kareen casually. 'Your writ does not extend so far, Protector of Books.'

'Your insolence is intolerable!' With a crackle and bang like the shutting of a weighty tome, Bikaj appeared, balancing on one of the tables in front of them. He was a weird sight indeed, for he manifested as an enormous caterpillar with many waving legs and arms, and a human sort of face, like a grey-whiskered, popping-eyed, furious old man with skin the colour of aged parchment. His long, fat segmented body was clothed in a kind of tunic and trousers edged in gold and turquoise, with a silk cloak flung over that, bordered with designs that resembled words and numbers. On his head he wore a fez-like cap with a gold bobble hanging down from it. He had an ivory hubble-bubble pipe clutched in one hand, which he drew on ferociously as he spoke.

'We keep a neat and ordered house here,' he snapped, regarding Kareen Amar with enormous disfavour, despite the fact she towered over him. 'Everything has its customary place. I myself, General Bikaj, command platoons of lesser Jinns which prevent the depredations of bookworms and silverfish and other bookish insects, thus earning us the undying gratitude of the family. We do not want any trouble caused by desert gypsies whose rank cannot even be determined.'

'General Bookworm,' said Kareen Amar sweetly, while Husam and Khaled listened, holding their breaths, 'let me remind you that it is we, the desert wanderers, who still have the greatest power, and the greatest prestige. You, my friend, have been given a small area in which to operate, and limited powers. You are safe that way, perhaps, from sorcerers who would not bother enslaving such as you; but remember, it was the desert Jinns, not the house ones, who went with the Messenger into the country of the angels. Remember your place, oh Master Bookworm. You are amongst a great deal of knowledge and wisdom here, but it does not seem to me you have absorbed much of it.'

Bikaj stared up at her, his eyes popping more than ever. 'Very well,' he said, in a deadly voice. 'I will remember my place. And that is to protect these books, and this library, in the house of al-Farouk.' He turned to Khaled, acknowledging him for the first time. 'Son of this house, I have always served the house of al-Farouk. It is not my role to answer the importunate questions of arrogant strangers.'

Kareen Amar's eye's flashed, but before she could speak again, Khaled interrupted. 'Will you answer my question, then, Lord Bikaj, as I am a son of this house, and you are bound to us?'

That was not the right thing to say. Bikaj drew up his fat body and said in an offended voice, 'We are not bound – we grant you our presence. And it should be the head of the al-Farouk household that asks the questions, not a junior member.'

'Stop your shillyshallying, Book-Jinn!' hissed Kareen Amar. 'We do not have time for your foolish niceties of protocol.'

'Well, then,' said Bikaj sharply, 'I do not have time for any foolish questions, either.'

'Wait,' said Khaled desperately, as Bikaj began to disappear, 'please, General Bikaj, I conjure you to answer my question. Though I am but a junior member of the house, still you have loyalty to my house. We want to wipe out the curse of Zohreh. Please, Lord Bikaj, if we do not, before my birthday in three days, I may well die and with me the house of al-Farouk, and even this library.'

Bikaj stopped in mid-disappearance, only his bewhiskered face hanging rather foolishly in the air. 'What is that you say?'

'I say that this is the hundredth anniversary of the curse, and on the hundredth anniversary the curse is at its most potent. You must know that, being so learned.' Bikaj nodded smugly. 'Well, then, dear General Bikaj, if the curse destroys me on my birthday, the al-Farouks will also be destroyed, this house abandoned, the library ruined.'

Bikaj's eyes started, and part of his body popped back into view. 'Why didn't you say so before, then? There is no time to be lost!'

'Yes, you fool,' snapped Kareen, 'why have you just realised that?'

'Son of the house,' said Bikaj, deliberately turning his back on Kareen, 'I fail to understand why you should employ such rude and discourteous servants.

And alas, I cannot tell you how to wipe out the curse of Zohreh, but I do know this: you must find where the Akamenian's talisman is hidden, in the arms of riddling Albalhol.'

'What? Where?' said Khaled.

'Listen! I haven't finished,' said Bikaj crossly. 'You must also go to the old graveyard of the al-Farouks, where Kassim is buried, for there some of the answer may be found. That is all I can tell you. I wish you good fortune.'

'Please, tell us more,' said Khaled hastily. But this time, Bikaj didn't linger. His voice floated on the air: 'I told you all I know, besides I have no wish to stay here and be insulted by a desert gypsy who thinks herself better than a General of Book-Jinns.'

After he'd vanished there was a short silence, then Kareen snapped, 'That fool really annoys me. I only just restrained myself from unleashing my fire against him!'

Khaled shivered. 'I'm glad you didn't,' he said softly, thinking of the curse.

'Wouldn't be the thing,' said Husam. 'Not in this place full of nice, flammable old books. Now, what about what he told us? Who or what is riddling Albalhol? And are we to speak with Kassim's ghost, in the graveyard?'

'I think we should discuss this outside, with the Shayk,' said Kareen Amar. 'I don't want to stay any longer in friend Bikaj's realm than is strictly necessary.

Khaled, are you coming?' she went on, frowning, as the youth showed a marked reluctance to follow them. 'Don't imagine you can get Bikaj back to talk to you, al-Farouk though you are; if I know such creatures, he'll be sulking over his offended dignity for weeks.'

Behind the curtain, Soheila stood frozen, stunned by what she had just heard. She made the sign of the Truthteller against her chest. A curse! Her ancestor had declared a curse against this wicked family.

She had come to the library because she'd had that dream again, in which the hooded figure beckoned her forward, but this time into the library. And so she had hurried here – and had learnt what she had learnt.

She'd been in the same room as a Jinn – as two Jinns! Her legs trembled, and for the first time since she had set out on her mission, she felt truly afraid. How could she fulfil her task if the al-Farouks had supernatural help, in addition to wealth and power? It appeared that they had the Talisman of the Star as well – for that must be the 'Akamenian's talisman' the Book-Jinn had referred to – though they had seemed to be unaware of its existence till then. And what was the curse? It didn't seem to have worked so far, if the al-Farouk's wealth and prosperity were any guide. But the boy – who must be the Al-Farouk heir – had spoken of the curse being most potent this year. It must be why she had had those dreams – Zohreh reaching across the barrier of time, and death, so that she could have one last certain chance of taking revenge.

She shivered, remembering her two encounters with the boy, in the garden and in the library. Would he tell his two dangerous friends about having met her there, and what she'd been doing? 'I will have to be very careful,' she thought, emerging from behind the curtain.

She must find out more. She must follow them to the graveyard, find out what was going on. But she must also find the Talisman of the Star for herself. What was it the creature had said: that the Talisman was held 'in the arms of riddling Albalhol'? She had no idea what that meant, but thought that the Talisman must be in here somewhere, for only then would Bikaj know about it at all. Yes, it must be somewhere in this library, and she was going to find it.

She glared determinedly at the ranks of shelves. 'By Akamenia and his prophet, the Truthteller,' she vowed, 'before too many days are out I will hold the ancient talisman of my family in my own hands.'

As she spoke the defiant words to herself, she happened to look over at the tall mirror that stood in the corner of the room. Her heart gave a great leap, for all at once she saw someone else reflected there: the hooded figure from her dream. Suddenly cold with fear, she whirled around. There was no-one in the room with her. No-one at all. But her nerves, already strained to breaking point, gave out at that moment, and she turned and fled from the room as fast as she could go.

Eleven

As the household sat down to breakfast, Soheila, standing in the shadows, listened as they decided the trip to the graveyard would be set for the next day, then she slipped back to the kitchen.

Today, Khaled would go under Husam's protection to the Carpet Bazaar, to find a repairer for the flying carpet, which might well be needed to travel long distances. Neither Abdullah nor Kareen would come with them, for they were to supervise another task — the search for the Talisman.

'I will call up all my clerical staff to help us. There is a catalogue of the books, you see,' said Abdullah, 'and we will start with that, with anything about Albalhol. We need to find out what that means, first of all, if we are to have a chance of finding the Talisman.'

'Do you have any idea what the Talisman might be?' said Husam.

Khaled looked a little warily at his father. 'There is

a story I read,' he said, 'which said that the clan Zohreh belonged to was named after a famous ancestor, the Magvanda Melkior, who obtained a magical object called the Talisman of the Star while on a mysterious journey to pay homage to a baby king whose coming had been foretold. They were guided there by a bright star, and angels.'

'That sounds like a Nashranee story my young friend Adi told me once,' said Husam. 'But Zohreh was not a Nashranee, was she?'

'No,' said the Shayk. 'She was an Akamenian. Fire-worshippers from Parsari.'

'Actually, Father,' said Khaled, 'they *don't* worship fire. That is an untruth put about by their enemies. Fire is just the symbol of their God, Akamenia. It is like saying we worship the Heaven Stone, instead of knowing it as a token from God.'

'The Light preserve us,' said Abdullah, after a short silence, 'the child presumes to teach theology now!'

Khaled said nothing. Husam said gently, 'I wonder then what exactly was the Talisman of the Star? Didn't it tell you, in this book of yours, Khaled?'

'No. It appears the Melkior clan have always closely guarded that secret.'

'Perhaps it's some kind of star chart, or instrument for looking at stars,' said Husam. He turned to Abdullah. 'Your ancestor Kassim must have hidden it, surely? Did he say nothing to anybody about it?'

'There is no record of it,' said Abdullah. 'I had no idea it existed, let alone that it was in my palace.' He sighed. 'Perhaps it was Zohreh herself who hid it; perhaps it's what holds the curse in place.'

'No,' said Kareen, speaking for the first time. 'I am sure it is Kassim who placed it there. If an enemy of the house had done so, the Jinn would know where it was. Bikaj only knows the riddle of where it was placed: a House-Jinn cannot penetrate to the heart of a family's secrets, for he or she is bound to a family and cannot betray it even inadvertently. I think that Bikaj told you all he knew.'

'Oh dear,' said Abdullah, 'I do wish Kassim had been a – nicer man. So much trouble could have been avoided. The old graveyard was abandoned because it was said ghouls haunted it. No-one was buried there after Kassim. We have a much nicer plot now. I haven't been to the old one in decades, not since I was your age, Khaled, and my father told me the story of the curse, standing at Kassim's grave.' He lowered his voice. 'It is said that Kassim's spirit is not in a good place, so I did not like being there, even though it was daylight. At night it is far too dangerous, with the ghouls having full power to prowl at their leisure.'

Khaled shivered. Ghouls are terrifying creatures. They are a kind of evil Jinn who haunt certain graveyards, particularly where wicked people are buried. They feed on dead flesh, but are not averse to sweet living flesh either.

If you come across one unawares, it will try to catch you, and tear you limb from limb, and eat your flesh.

'But ghouls can be defeated with a stout heart and a trust in the Light,' Khaled said, in a rush, 'so there's nothing really to be afraid of, especially in daylight. I should like to defeat one myself.'

Abdullah and Husam looked at each other. Husam said, 'Have you ever seen a ghoul, Khaled?'

'No, but —'

'I hope to God you never do, my son,' said Abdullah gravely.

'Indeed,' said Husam, 'ghouls are no laughing matter, at any time.'

'Ghouls!' said Kareen, with great scorn. 'They are evil things, but they hold no terror for me, sordid and stupid things that they are.'

That made everyone laugh, and lightened the tension a little.

On the way to the Carpet Bazaar, Husam and Omar chatted animatedly about Jayangan — or rather, Omar asked questions and Husam answered, at great length. Khaled listened to them, fascinated. He would like, one day, to travel the world; it was so big, and so much of it was worth seeing. He liked the sound of Jayangan, and of Husam's friends, Dewi and Adi, who were about his age. He wished they could have come with Husam; he had few friends of his own age, for his exalted rank made things very difficult indeed for him here. But in another country, he'd just be Khaled, not the heir to the vast al-Farouk fortune and the ancient al-Farouk name. He could be himself. One day, perhaps, he might visit them with Husam. One day, when all this was over and he could breathe again. 'One day,' he thought with a shock of fear, 'if I make it past my fifteenth birthday . . .'

All at once, for no reason that he could discern, the face of the Parsarian kitchen boy came into his mind. He thought suddenly that he should have asked Payem some questions; if he was an Akamenian, he might know things that could be of help. Yet the boy had not actually admitted to being an Akamenian, so what was he doing in the library, looking at a book of Akamenian legends? Unease stirred at the back of Khaled's mind. Maybe he should ask Husam's advice. But he didn't want to get the boy into any trouble. He liked him. He felt oddly protective towards him, strangely drawn to him, though the boy was only a servant.

The car stopped. They had arrived at the Carpet Bazaar. Husam and Khaled got out, leaving Omar with the car.

The bazaar was a huge market under a great arched roof whose ceiling was covered in gold and glass tiles, and whose walls were painted cream, picked out in crimson and purple and gold. Graceful galleries lined the walls right up to the ceiling, and the floors were of beautiful white and blue mosaics. A winding mahogany staircase led to each gallery in turn, with its multitude of carpet shops. There were large shops and small ones, selling carpets from every corner of the el 'Jisal world, and even beyond: carpets in every gradation of colour, beauty, style and price, made from silk and wool and goat-hair and cotton, ranging from simple tribal mats to magnificent rarities fit for the audience chamber of a king. Some shops specialised in carpets with abstract designs, others in story-carpets richly depicting scenes from legend or history. Some of the shops had importunate middlemen outside them, harassing them to come in and try, look, buy! Others had haughty guards standing outside, as if the premises were some kind of lord's chamber you needed permission to enter.

Of course, Khaled was recognised by several of the sellers. Many curious eyes followed the two as they made their way up the galleries, Husam carrying the flying carpet, carefully wrapped up, under his arm.

The Mesomian's shop was at the far end of the top gallery, tucked away behind a pillar. It was a small but smart shop, with the name 'Harir and Sons' – the name Farasha had referred to – painted in discreet golden letters on the door. It appeared closed, however, for the light was not on, and the door was locked. Khaled and Husam were looking at each other, bitterly disappointed, when a soft voice hailed them. 'Psst!'

They looked around but could see nobody. 'Psst!' said the voice again, and a crooked finger emerged from the other side of the furthest pillar, in the dusty shadows of the stairwell, beckoning. 'Come here, friends.' The voice spoke in Aksaran, with a strong Alhindi accent. They looked at each other, then Husam said bluntly, 'Who are we speaking to?'

'You seek Harir, do you not?'

'Yes, but –'

'Come over here, sir, please, you will not regret it,' said the voice. 'I am a friend, who can help you. I know you seek a carpet repairer. And I know you have a magic carpet, a carpet that is essential to your task.'

Husam looked at Khaled. Grimly, he clapped a hand to his side. 'I'm armed,' he whispered. 'If he tries any funny business, he'll regret it.'

Khaled remembered that this man had been the Sultan's Chief Executioner. 'Let's go and see who he is, and what he wants, then.'

Twelve

In the shadows, a strange little man was crouching. He was almost a dwarf, with a large head on a thin neck and a short, squat body. He had weathered skin the colour and consistency of old leather, and the biggest, thickest pepper-and-salt moustache they'd ever seen, which ate up half his face. He wore a dirty brown turban on his head; his trousers and shirt had clearly seen better days; and his dusty feet were thrust into clumsy rubber sandals of the kind only the poor wore. In one gnarled hand, he clutched a hessian bag. He beckoned to them. In his singsong Alhindi voice, he whispered, 'Come closer, come closer. There is something you must hear. You must not go to Mr Harir's shop.'

They stared at him. Khaled was the first to recover. 'Who are you? Why do you tell us this?'

For answer, the Alhindi grinned and rolled up the right sleeve of his shirt. On his arm was strapped a dozen or so watches, of the cheap kind that imitate famous brands; he rolled up his other sleeve, and there, tied on with little ribbons, were an equal number of cheap sunglasses. He then held out his bag, and dived a hand into it, pulling out three or four mobile phones, made of cheap coloured plastic. 'You see, my friends?'

'Are you telling me you lured us here just to sell us your cheap rubbish?' said Khaled, with great scorn.

'Don't be hasty, master,' said the old dwarf, smiling. 'These are not what they seem. I am a Jinn master from Alhind, and house my Jinns in these trinkets. My name is Sharib.'

Khaled stared at him, baffled, but Husam's face cleared. 'I have heard of people like you. I have never met one, though.' He turned to Khaled. 'The people of Alhind have some unusual magic. Jinn masters are only found there.'

'I don't understand. Do you enslave Jinns to do your bidding?' frowned Khaled.

The Alhindi sighed. 'No, no. I am not a sorcerer, enslaving afreets and the like. I tame and teach minor Jinns. Your friend is right; it is a calling peculiar to my country. You see, long ago, one of my ancestors married a Jinn woman and this has given us a special place, and special powers. We do not deal in black magic. We do not try to enslave the powerful old Jinns, the free spirits, whether good or bad – that is far too dangerous, dark work. But there are others, less important, less powerful, not terribly bright, but still useful, who can be taught and persuaded to help human beings, each in their limited way.'

'Oh,' said Khaled, 'I had never heard of such a thing.'

'Well, now you have,' said Sharib tartly. 'My young friend, there is a niche for every Jinn, somewhere. But changing times means new skills need to be learnt, if they are to continue to be useful to their human hosts. I have found ways of training some of the lesser Jinns to function in our modern world. And I am here to help you now because, well, that is how I earn my living, besides selling trumpery rubbish. And I think you need help such as mine?' He looked up at Husam. 'I can see that you, sir, have walked closely with Jinns and other spirits, and I can see that you, sir,' he went on, turning to Khaled, 'are in great trouble of mind. You are facing a great test. You are in danger. And you need help.'

'How do you know that?' said Khaled.

'I will show you how in a little while,' said Sharib, grinning. 'And you will see how I can help you, too. Now, whom do I have the honour of addressing?'

It was a salesman's quick and easy patter, but there was something fascinating and convincing about the cheerful dwarf. Khaled smiled. 'My name is Khaled bin Abdullah al-Farouk; this is my father's friend and now mine, Husam al-Din, who is visiting us from Jayangan.'

'Pleased to meet you both,' said Sharib, bowing rather comically. 'Al-Farouk, eh! I have heard of your family. Your father's on the Ameeratan Governing Council, eh, that right? Thought so. A great lord then, close to the Prince. I am honoured to meet you, sir, and your friend.' He was all but rubbing his hands in glee. If he earnt his living as a Jinn master then he must think he'd fallen on worthwhile customers indeed in the al-Farouks. 'Now, then,' he went on, 'to show you my qualifications.' He rummaged in his bag and triumphantly held up a phone. 'As you no doubt know, tame Jinn can be summoned through a ring of power or a lamp. But these days, other objects can help to summon a useful Jinn, unnoticed by all.' He waggled the phone around. 'Behold the Jinn of distant hearing. No matter where you might be, in the desert or at the bottom of the sea, this Jinn will let you hear even the quietest conversation.' He pressed a button and the phone's panel lit up. A thin voice wailed, 'I am the Jinn of the Phone, Master, and your humble apprentice. Whose words do you desire to hear?'

Sharib grinned, took a quick look over the balcony and said, 'The fat lady with the blue veil near the shop of that Parsarian crook Massoud, what is she saying, oh Jinn of the Phone?'

The panel flashed, then the voice took on a different tone, the tone of a woman used to commanding people: 'I want a better price than that. You told me yesterday you were keeping a special one for me. What is this nonsense, boy? Get me your master at once, I demand to speak with him!'

Smiling at Husam's and Khaled's wide eyes, Sharib turned off the phone. He carefully untied one of the pairs of sunglasses he wore on his arm. He held them up and touched the sides of the glasses. 'Behold the Jinn of far-seeing.' The glass clouded, and a whispery, breathy voice said, 'I am the Jinn of the Glasses, Master, and your humble apprentice. What is it you wish to see?'

'If you put on these glasses and ask the Jinn a question about an object,' said Sharib, 'it will tell you what you need to know.' He folded the sunglasses away. 'I was intrigued by that big parcel you carry under your arm, Husam al-Din. I asked the Jinn of the Glasses a question. And I learnt you have there a flying carpet, made in the Marshlands of Mesomia. I knew too it had malfunctioned in some way. I knew it was important to you. Thus I knew you were headed to Harir's shop.'

'Now this,' went on the dwarf, unstrapping a rather shabby plastic watch from his right arm, 'is something else. Behold the Jinn of time.' He pressed the knob on the side of the watch. Instantly a deep voice whispered, 'I am the Jinn of the Watch, Master, and your humble apprentice. Where in time do you wish to go?'

Khaled and Husam stared at Sharib. 'Can it really take you back in time?' whispered Khaled.

'Well,' said Sharib, 'it doesn't actually take you bodily there, you understand. But it will show you what happened at a particular time.' He pressed the knob of the watch again and said, 'Jinn of the Watch, show me what was happening here today, on this spot, at the precise time of nine am.'

'I obey,' said the Jinn, and instantly, the face of the watch clouded, then cleared again. Crowding around it, they saw that the numbers and hands of the watch face had disappeared; instead it had become like a tiny television screen. And in the screen, they could see the spot where they were standing. It was quite empty of people.

'Nothing happening then,' said Sharib, deftly flicking the knob. The screen went blank again; then the face of the watch, with its numbers and hands, returned. 'I have to confess I haven't sorted out everything with this one,' said the dwarf. 'It can only reach up to two or three hours back in time, and in a narrow location. Still, it's a good start.'

'Are all those phones and glasses and watches you carry actually Jinn?' said Khaled, open-mouthed.

'Oh no,' said Sharib, 'they're not actually Jinn, in themselves. They just provide habitation for certain sorts of Jinns – ones who cannot manifest with a body of their own but must be contained within some material thing. And only those three items I showed you are House-Jinns. The others are cheap rubbishy objects, merely there to hide the real ones.' He grinned. 'And also to sell – they do earn me a little pocket money when I cannot find appropriate clients for my Jinn skills.

'For more than a year now, due to certain – er – unfortunate adventures when one of my Jinns didn't quite do what it was supposed to do, and caused me grief with a mighty patron, I have been living here, having thought it prudent to leave a little distance between myself and Alhind for a while, till things died down.' He gave an engaging grin. 'Now then. You wanted to speak to Harir, about your malfunctioning flying carpet, yes?' His bright gaze was on the parcel under Husam's arm.

They looked at each other then nodded.

'Harir is dead,' said Sharib. 'As you know, he was a Mesomian refugee. He was murdered last night, betrayed to The Vampire's spies by one of his associates. He was known to have links to the resistance against The Vampire, and to be skilled in the repair of Mesomian flying carpets. The Vampire means to control the production of flying carpets as well as wiping out any resistance to his rule. He both fears and is obsessed with any form of magic. He has gangs of sorcerers and practitioners of black magic living in his palaces, working for him. Anyone who practises good magic has been killed, exiled, or in the case of the Carpet Enchantresses of the Marshlands, has fled to remote places. The Vampire's spies will be watching Harir's shop now. Anyone who comes to the shop bearing a genuine carpet from the Enchantresses will be in big trouble. We should probably leave right away.'

He cocked his head to one side and made a sudden grab for the parcel under Husam's arm. Husam stumbled back and dropped the carpet, with a shout.

'Shush, shush,' said Sharib, a finger to his lips. 'You brought a spy with you.' He began to hum – a strange, tuneless, soft yet metallic-sounding hum for all the world like a mosquito's whine. With one hand, he described a little circle in the air in front of the parcel, as if he were scribbling. And suddenly, in the middle of this circle, appeared, as if it were suddenly pulled out of a bottle, a small, plump moth-like creature with a cross human face.

Khaled gasped, 'The Light preserve us, it's Farasha!'

'Farasha,' repeated Sharib, a stern expression in his eyes. 'You have brought your own pet Jinn with you. Why?'

'He most certainly has not,' piped a thin, indignant voice. Farasha's expression would have been most forbidding if it hadn't been comical.

'He's not my pet,' Khaled said in a resigned voice. 'You're offending him, Sharib.'

'That he is,' said Farasha. 'I have never been so offended in my life. I, Farasha of the great clan of Yaka-bikaj, am the guardian Jinn of the Repository of Highly Important Books at the House of Al-Farouk.'

'Oh, is that what you are?' said Sharib, suddenly grinning. 'A member of a cosy House-Jinn clan, eh? Well, mind out I don't grab you and put you to work for me, my little friend. Highly Important Books, eh? I doubt it. You come from some forgotten storeroom somewhere, yes? If you were so important in the House-Jinn caste I think you'd have stayed at home and sent a minion in your place. So you're the minion, right?'

'Most assuredly not!' said Farasha, even more indignantly. 'I came of my own accord, to see what these people were doing, in case they were meddling with things that would bring disgrace on our house. It was I who told them about Harir the carpet repairer; it was my important information that got them here in the first place, Alhindi Jinn master.'

Sharib laughed. 'I don't believe it! A House-Jinn, and a minion at that, with his own initiative. What is the world coming to? Very well, Farasha the Spy, you may stay, but no funny tricks, you understand, or it's into a bottle with you. I could use another tame Jinn, you know.'

'I'd like to see you try,' said Farasha, with great dignity but a certain unsteadiness in his voice. It was apparent that he was not altogether sure of his ground with the dwarf.

'Don't tempt me,' said Sharib, eyes twinkling. 'Now then, let us go. There is someone you must meet – a friend of mine who is also a very good carpet repairer. He does not work here, but at the Gold Market. Come on,' he said, seeing their hesitation, 'you really need to get that carpet fixed, it is important to your task. My Jinns have told me so.'

Thirteen

It was not very far from the Carpet Bazaar to the Gold Market. As soon as the car stopped, Sharib jumped out with great alacrity. 'I had better get on ahead of you,' he said. 'You see, my friend can be a trifle unpredictable at times, and doesn't like to be taken unawares. I will meet you in the Ali Baba Emporium in five minutes. Okay?' And without waiting for an answer, he scurried off as fast as his short legs would allow him.

Husam and Khaled looked at each other. 'I'm not sure I like this at all,' said Husam, slowly. 'Perhaps you had better stay here with Omar, Khaled.'

'I think that might be wise,' said the driver. 'Street sellers are often rogues.'

'I am going,' said Khaled haughtily. 'He said it was important to our task.'

Husam met his eyes, and sighed. 'Very well. But you must not hesitate if I tell you to run, Khaled. Do you understand?'

'Take my gun,' said Omar, pulling his weapon out
of the glove-box. 'If all else fails . . .'

'We can't start shooting in the middle of the Gold
Market,' said Husam, shaking his head. 'Don't worry,
Omar. I have a good sword, and a swift hand. If anyone
tries anything . . .' He smiled, and made a cutting
gesture across his throat.

The Gold Market was not quite as big as the
Carpet Bazaar, but every bit as extraordinary. A wide,
mosaic-floored aisle ran between two rows of small
shops, behind whose large windows sparkled, glittered, glowed and shone hundreds, thousands, of
pieces of jewellery, mostly of heavy yellow gold, set
with bright gemstones. There were also shops selling
statues and carvings, in pure gold and rock crystal and
marble and ebony and ivory; shops selling gold and
silver and platinum watches, some set with diamonds
and rubies and emeralds; and discreet banking shops
where you could trade suitcases full of paper money
for gold bars.

The Ali Baba Emporium, despite its grand name,
was a narrow, rather shabby shop at the far end of the
market. There was only one shop assistant in it, and no
customers. The shop assistant, a neat young Alhindi in
a dark suit, beckoned them in rather nervously. 'Please,
you are to come this way,' he said, ushering them
rapidly to the back of the shop. He pulled aside a long
curtain on the back wall, revealing a heavy-looking

wooden door. With an anxious smile, he opened the door. 'Please, you come in here.'

His hand on his sword, Husam growled, 'Now wait a moment. What is in there?'

The shop assistant whispered, 'You go in there.'

'Stop repeating yourself,' said Husam. Drawing his sword, he stepped cautiously through the doorway, Khaled hot on his heels.

They were in a dim, dusty storage room, with another door at one end. Sharib was standing by that door, looking rather impatient. 'Come on. Shut the door.'

'What's all the mystery?' said Husam, advancing on him, his sword still drawn. He scanned the room, but it was empty of anything except for Sharib and a few boxes. 'Who are we going to meet?'

'You'll see. I'm sorry,' said the Jinn master, smiling placatingly, 'but it's got to be this way. My friend is very wary. There is a price on his head, in Mesomia. The Vampire's agents have been looking for him for a long time. And he has certain other – er – problems.' He looked earnestly at Husam and Khaled and went on, 'I tell you, he is important to you because he is now the only one in Jumana who can repair your carpet. And it must be repaired, or Khaled may be in the very gravest danger.'

Husam frowned. Before he could say anything, Khaled cut in. 'Husam, I have very little time. I must have all the help I can possibly get. We need to follow up every single lead. And you are here to protect me. You have your sword, and you know how to deal with Jinn. We must take the chance. You must see that!'

'Hmm,' said Husam, looking from one to the other. 'Very well. But don't try any funny business, Sharib. I won't hesitate to kill you if you betray us.'

'I'm sure you wouldn't,' said the Alhindi, 'and I value my head, friend Husam. Besides, Khaled is right. You must try everything. You don't have the luxury of picking and choosing, when it comes to defeating strong magic.' He paused. 'Now, I have to explain to you: we are going to go through this door here, which leads to a strongroom, where my friend will be waiting. You will have to be blindfolded. I'm sorry, friend Husam, but it must be so.'

'Please, Husam,' said Khaled, warningly.

'Well, I'm not leaving my sword behind for any-thing,' said Husam. 'And I'm warning you: blindfolded or not, I can still cut you in ribbons.'

'I know that,' said Sharib, smiling faintly. 'Now then, if we're agreed, we've got to get going, and quickly. For each of you, I have a scarf to tie over your eyes. There is also a rope, which you are each to hang on to. Once you are ready, I will escort you to where my friend is. You are to keep on the blindfold the whole time you are in his presence. Agreed?'

Slowly, they nodded.

'Good,' said Sharib. 'You won't regret it.'

As Khaled tied the blindfold around his eyes, he felt a soft fluttering near his right ear. 'Oh, dear, oh dear,' came Farasha's anxious whisper. 'Where exactly are we going?'

Khaled said nothing, because what could he have answered? Perhaps they were going into a trap.

'Right, all ready? Off we go!' The rope gave a jerk, and Husam and Khaled stumbled unseeingly after Sharib. 'Now then. Here's the first door,' came the dwarf's cheerful voice. 'Step through. That's right. Now a few steps down. Careful, don't slip. Another door, and then we'll be there.'

They could hear a bolt being drawn across. The rope jerked a little more, then stopped. 'Drop the rope now,' Sharib said. 'Remember: do not try and take off your blindfold.'

They heard the slap of Sharib's rubber sandals on what sounded like a concrete floor; they heard the murmur of voices, at some distance, then coming closer; and at the same time, they heard the sound of another pair of footsteps beside Sharib's, sliding along as if their owner were crippled in some way. They could smell a rank smell, overlaid with the heady fumes of kalfkat, a powerful herb. But they could see nothing.

'Welcome,' said a voice. It was a soft, dark, velvety man's voice. Khaled felt the hairs on his arms rise up, for it seemed to him as if the material of his blindfold was thinning out, gradually, till it was like a kind of pale mist over his eyes: a mist in which he could, at first vaguely, then more clearly, see forms emerging.

They were in a room lit only by a warm, glowing lamp. There was a big safe against one wall, a shelf with ledgers on it, a workbench with tools scattered on it and a tall water pipe, from which wafted a thin stream of kalfkat smoke. Husam's hand still gripped his sword. Over there was Sharib's squat form and beside him – dear God, what was it – a hulking male form, wrapped in black, whose face seemed to be nearly all covered in what looked like shaggy brown hair, with a strange lock of pure white hair at the front. Only the eyes were visible under all the hair: almond-shaped, amber-coloured eyes with black, spiky lashes, the pupils narrowed under the influence of kalfkat. Khaled could see that the man held himself stiffly, painfully upright, as though, he thought suddenly, he would prefer to go on all fours. It was a beast – or a man that looked like a beast. He couldn't help make a gulping sound, and then heard Farasha whisper, right near his ear. 'Quiet! Quiet! He must not know I am helping you to see. Act as if you can't see.'

So that was the explanation for the sudden way he could see under his blindfold. Khaled gulped again, and struggled to control himself. 'My name is Gur Thalab al Kutroob. My friend Sharib has told me what you need. Please give me the carpet, that I may examine it.'

Through the thin mist over his eyes, Khaled could see, as if in the muddied reflection in a stream, hands stretching out for the carpet Husam was holding out: hands that were almost paws, big, square, hairy, yet set with magnificent rings. Then he saw the creature and Sharib bending over the carpet; he could hear an unintelligible murmur. At his shoulder, Farasha was silent, though Khaled could feel his tension. Husam, too, was silent, holding himself stiffly, every muscle stilled.

Sharib got to his feet. 'My friend confirms that your carpet is indeed a rare thing. It was made by a Mesomian Carpet Enchantress – but a very young one. She had too many ideas and did not finish the piece properly. He thinks he can fix it, but it may take some time, for at present he is not well. You will have to come back in three days.'

'Three days!' said Khaled, before he could stop himself. 'But we have just over three days before I –' He broke off abruptly as the hairy head turned sharply towards him, the amber eyes glittering with an alien shine. At the same moment, Husam moved swiftly in front of Khaled, blocking any action the creature might take. There was a heartbeat of tense silence, then the beautiful voice said, very softly, 'Before you what?'

'Lord,' came Sharib's voice, no longer cheerful but

full of a barely repressed anxiety, 'he is a boy. He does not know how to –'

'Let him speak,' said the beast.

Khaled said, 'Forgive my impatience, but I am under a curse, and if I do not break it before three days are up, I will die. And my family name will die with me. Sharib has told us the carpet may help to save me, and that you are the one who can repair it. Will you help us?'

There was silence, then the beast said, 'I will try. But if you are cursed, then so am I, with a curse nothing and no-one can ever break. And today is not a good day for me, so it will take time.' The amber eyes glittered fiercely, the hands that were almost paws clenched around each other close to the creature's chest, as if they were crushing something – or as if they were pre-venting the creature from leaping on the humans. 'Now go. You have been here a long time already, and I am afraid I will not be able to leash the beast inside me for too much longer. It is good you wore those blindfolds; it is never good for me to meet others' eyes in this state.' The eyes rested on Khaled for a shivery instant. Khaled looked straight ahead, as if he were truly blind under the scarf. His heart pounded like a drum.

'Here's the rope,' came Sharib's voice, very brisk. 'Hold on and follow me.' He took them almost at a run through the door, which he slammed shut, then up the stairs, and back through the next door, which he closed with a clang and locked and bolted as soon as they were through. It was then that they heard the long, mournful wolf's howl, wafting up from down below: a howl of fury and grief, of frustration and despair and a deep, deep sorrow that made their blood feel as if it were turned to ice.

'You may take off your blindfolds now,' said Sharib. He sounded tired, and rather breathless. 'It's safe, don't worry. Good, that's done. It's always a little bit – er – edgy when my friend is in one of his bad moods.'

'The Light preserve us,' said Husam. Khaled noticed there was sweat on his forehead. 'You took us to meet a *werewolf*. No wonder you were so secretive and jumpy.'

'He is under the werewolf curse, but he is a good man,' said Sharib earnestly. 'He's the son of an Arga, a prince from the beautiful green Kirtis Mountains of Mesomia, and in his family the werewolf curse visits every other generation. He should have been the heir, but renounced his claim, fearing the thing in his blood would make him too dangerous. He left his home and ended up in the armed resistance against The Vampire, hiding out in the Marshlands, where he learnt carpet repair from the Enchantresses. It did not help his family: his father the Arga was murdered by his own brother with the help of The Vampire, and took the Kirtis throne by force. Gur Thalab was betrayed by one of his own kinsmen and was captured by The Vampire's agents and taken to the notorious Black Prison, where he was foully tortured. But somehow he managed to escape, and found refuge here.' He sighed. 'Poor Gur Thalab. Poor Mesomia. But that is not your concern, friends. Your carpet will be in good hands. And it's quite likely he'll have it ready before it's needed.'

'Do you think so?' asked Khaled anxiously.

'I am sure.' Sharib peered rather owlishly at them. 'Now, then, what are we to do? It is in my mind I could help you, too, to break this curse of yours, for my Jinns may well be useful to you.'

Khaled said, 'Oh yes, I think that you should come with us, Sharib, back home, to meet Father and Kareen Amar. Don't you think so, Husam?'

'I suppose so,' said Husam, a little grudgingly.

Sharib smiled and rubbed his hands in great satisfaction. 'I am glad to be working at my real job again. Heavens! If you only knew how dull it is to try and wheedle people into buying trumpery rubbish. Lead on, Khaled bin Abdullah – I will follow you wherever you want me to go.'

Omar frowned mightily when he heard that the ragged little street seller was actually coming back with them to the palace. Though he did not say anything, it was plain he was more than disapproving. As he drove along he kept glancing at the seat beside him, as if checking that Sharib wasn't vandalising the car or stealing some fixture. Sharib didn't seem to care, he was too busy chatting with the others. Which was why nobody noticed the motorbike following them at a discreet distance, all the way back from the Gold Market.

That evening, Khaled went to bed early, exhausted in every way. But he lay awake for ages, worrying over their lack of progress, and the way the clock was steadily ticking towards the fateful day. His father and the clerks had, so far, discovered nothing about the Talisman's hiding place at all; and he might have to wait for days for the carpet to be fixed. Meanwhile, Kareen had vanished on some lead of her own, and Sharib's Jinns had turned up nothing of any consequence in the library. Indeed, they appeared unable to function in there at all, perhaps because Bikaj was somehow hindering them, out of spite.

He would have been even more worried if he had been in the library at the stroke of midnight. Soheila, summoned again by her insistent dream, stood in front of the tall carved mirror, holding the silk sachet in which lay Zohreh's ashes. She was pale as death, shaking all over, but trying hard to be brave.

'Zohreh, Grandmother of Grandmothers, I am here. It is I, your descendant, Soheila. Will you not speak to me?'

The mirror began to cloud over but Soheila could see nothing in it, not even the hooded figure. 'Grandmother of Grandmothers, honoured Zohreh, please speak to me. I need your help, if I am to do my duty.'

It felt to her as if the very air were freezing over. Her teeth chattered in her head.

The hooded figure suddenly materialised in the misted mirror. Soheila could not see the figure's face, but knew it was staring straight at her. She whispered, 'Please, are you Zohreh?'

The figure did not move, but it seemed to get larger, more menacing, more dominating. Soheila's hands shook so much that the sachet fell on the floor. She bent down to pick it up, and as she did so, suddenly the hooded figure in the mirror moved. The hood was thrown back and Soheila found herself staring into the most terrifying face she had ever seen. It was an inhuman face – lipless, hairless, the colour of ash, but with two burning, glittering eyes of a startling blue-green, just like her own. The horrid lipless mouth moved, but Soheila heard not a word. She had fainted.

She came to a couple of minutes later and sprang to her feet, cursing her own weakness and fear. But it was too late; the mirror had cleared. The figure had gone. Clutching the ashes, she whispered, 'Come back. Come back. Forgive me,' but nothing happened. Her ancestor had gone. Perhaps she would never appear to her again.

Heart wrung by guilt, regret and sorrow, she crept back along the passages to the servants' quarters. She slept very badly that night, and woke early so that she could stow away in the car bound for the al-Farouk graveyard.

Fourteen

Morning, and the big shiny four-wheel-drive car bounced along the highway, heading for the turn-off to the disused desert road that led to the old al-Farouk cemetery. In the back, hidden under blankets, Soheila hardly dared breathe. The effect of the previous night had not quite worn off, and she felt exhausted, her eyes gritty, her throat constricted. But she was determined that this time she would not show any fear, no matter what horrors lurked in that graveyard.

She felt a measure of faint relief at knowing that at least the wicked man who had so foully murdered her innocent ancestress did not lie in honour, but in a deserted place, and that even his kinsmen were afraid to visit his burial place. Ghouls did not frighten her – they had no place in the stories of her own people – but what of the ghost of Kassim, if it should appear? She offered several prayers to Akamenia to protect her, and made the sign of the Truthteller to seal them. She had not brought Zohreh's ashes with her. The graveyard was a place of unclean spirits, the resting place of a wicked man. Who knew what evil things might be there, to sully her ancestor's honoured remains? She had failed Zohreh last night; she did not want to fail her again.

The car lurched to a stop. Soheila could hear the murmur of conversation; she did not dare poke up her head just yet. Then car doors slammed. Cautiously Soheila lifted her head up, and slid, the dark blanket still wrapped around her, to the back window. The vehicle had tinted reflective windows of the kind that are easy enough to see out of but not see into — perfect for anonymity in traffic, and also for Soheila's purposes. She peered out and saw low dunes of sand, and a solitary large thorn tree, under whose tortured spreading branches was what must be the old cemetery: an enclave surrounded by a tall, crumbling mud wall, with a heavy metal gate set into it. Faded signs against the evil eye were painted on the metal: an attempt to ensure that whatever foul thing was inside *stayed* inside.

Once the others went through that gate, Soheila would see nothing. She had to follow them. But how, without being seen? She looked at the thorn tree and had an idea. Part of its massive trunk grew outside the cemetery wall; if she climbed up it, into the branches, she would see what was happening down below whilst being unseen.

Soheila breathed another prayer to Akamenia, opened the rear door, and very cautiously slipped out of the car. She hid for a second behind the sand dune closest to the car, then peered around and saw that the driver was making his way back to the car, where, presumably, he would wait. She ducked behind the sand dune and looked out. The driver had pulled down the car shades. He wouldn't see her. The others had already reached the cemetery. It was safe for her to move. She crawled as carefully as she could, round the back of the dune, till she reached the thorn tree.

She shinned up the tree and quickly reached the top of the wall. She looked down into a strange and desolate place indeed. Broken grey marble headstones, dead twigs from the thorn tree and what looked horribly like bits of bones lay scattered on the sandy ground. In the very centre stood a tall, polished red marble headstone. Somehow this was the most horrid sight of all, for it stood almost undamaged amongst the desolation around it, the very sand around it quite undisturbed. There was nothing written on the stone – if there had been once, it had vanished – but Soheila knew instantly it was the headstone of Kassim himself.

Down below, Abdullah and Husam and Khaled were standing at a cautious distance from the headstone, deep in conversation. The Jinn Kareen Amar prowled around the further reaches of the cemetery, sniffing at the air, her hands held out in front of her, groping, feeling for unseen presences. The Jinn's eyes were glowing bright red; her mouth was set in a thin line, and an eerie warning whistle was coming from it; her hair seemed almost electric. It was obvious there were *things* there – things that so far were not choosing to manifest themselves.

Soheila felt an urgent, shameful desire to clamber down from her post, run back to the car and hide under the blankets. She silently told herself: 'You're scared before anything's even happened, you fool, you coward. You will stay here; you will not hide or run or faint; you will be steadfast, strong as a rock.'

She tore her attention away from the Jinn and concentrated instead on the men and the boy. Husam's features were set in an expressionless mask and he appeared to be quite calm; but there was a faint sheen of sweat on both Khaled's and Abdullah's brows, and a staring quality about their eyes which told a story of rigid self-control. Abdullah had one arm around his son. 'Kareen,' he called out softly, in a voice that tried to be steady, 'what is it you feel?'

The Jinn whirled around to him, her hair standing quite on end, her face suffused with a red glow. Her voice came out as a low growl. 'They will let you speak. Speak quickly, though.'

Abdullah gently released his son, handing him over to Husam's care. 'Do not be afraid,' he said. Khaled nodded, gulped. Something evil, truly evil, was here, he knew. He hardly noticed how he clutched at Husam's hand. He said prayers under his breath, prayers for all of them, but especially for his father.

'Great-great-great-grandfather Kassim,' said Abdullah, clutching his walking-stick and bowing his head very low so that he appeared to be speaking to the sand at his feet, 'we come today to ask of you one thing. Will you speak with us?'

'Necromancy,' thought Soheila, clutching desperately at the tree. 'He means to ask his wicked ancestor for help in finally destroying their already defeated enemies.' Burning hatred filled her heart to the exclusion of all else, except fear.

Kareen Amar came back to their side. She stood very close to the headstone, her head up, her eyes roaming everywhere, as if she were on guard. But she said nothing.

'Will you speak with us?' repeated Abdullah, his voice cracking this time, his hands shaking.

Silence. And then Soheila, her hair standing on end, her hands suddenly growing icy, heard an ominous cracking sound. The red headstone rocked, the sand at its base opened, and *something* flowed out of the sudden, yawning darkness underneath – something whose form and features could not at first be properly discerned for it was clothed in a kind of clinging grey mist, but whose very presence was wrong, oppressive, terrifying. With the apparition came a terrible stink – a cloying, horrible thing that seemed to sink into Soheila's very pores, making her feel unclean, defiled, breathless with horror and disgust. And then came the voice, and somehow that was far worse than anything. It was a woman's voice, sweet and musical on the surface, but with a depth of darkness and evil in it that was unlike anything Soheila could ever have imagined.

'Who disturbs the burial place of Kassim?' The clinging grey mist shook and shimmered, the form behind it beginning slowly, slowly to take shape. Meanwhile, Abdullah, Khaled and Husam stood rigid, apparently quite unable to move, just like Soheila. Kareen Amar seemed unaffected, for it was she who replied.

'You know very well who it is, Grabber,' she said harshly. 'You also know very well that for them to speak to you their names would give you power over them. But it is I, Kareen Amar, songstress of the Jinn, ancient and wild spirit of much higher rank than your worm-ridden sort of vile ghoul, who does call on you now, and puts you under the binding of our kind: you must answer one question, honestly, and without any tricks.'

The Grabber shrieked, 'Kareen Amar! I have heard of you. You are a deceiver and a traitor to our kind, a lover of corrupt humanity.'

'Say what you like, Grabber,' said Kareen Amar coldly. 'You have no power over me. Now, I bind you to answer one question these people will pose to you. You know that unless you want to follow Iblis into Jehannem, you must answer it.'

'One only then,' shrieked the voice, sweet no longer, but horrid with vile, disappointed fury. The mist cleared and Soheila found herself staring down at a horrible creature, more horrible than anything she could have imagined, far worse than her ancestor's ghost in the mirror. The ghoul had a hyena's ugly head and bone-cracking jaws, from the corners of which blood-flecked spittle ran; raised, stiff hair on its shoulders; and, horrifyingly, a woman's slender body, clothed in gauzy grey robes, from under which long, hideous clawed feet peered. The ghoul's hands, though delicate and long-fingered, ended in curved yellow claws, and these were extended longingly towards Kareen Amar as it turned its ugly head to stare at her companions. Abdullah and Husam each placed a hand on Khaled's shoulders, framing him, holding him desperately within their own warmth. It was all they could do.

The ghoul known as the Grabber moved slowly, in a jerky motion, towards Husam, Khaled and Abdullah, its hyena's eyes glowing with a pale, cold yellow fire. As it moved, the death-stink intensified with every step. For the first time, Soheila felt pity and even a certain reluctant admiration for the men and boy below, having to stand there and let that thing come close to them. She knew that if it had been her facing it directly, looking into its eyes, she would not have been able to resist the temptation to run away. She could only imagine what it cost them to stand unmoving in the face of the creature. What she didn't know was that at least for Khaled, it was actually impossible to move. He was beyond fear, beyond terror, numb and para-lysed, the only trace of warmth Husam's hand on one shoulder, his father's on the other.

'Well?' said the ghoul. Kareen Amar moved a little closer to the men. The Grabber's eyes flashed. 'Keep a distance, Kareen Amar,' it said, and its pink, whip-thin tongue flicked out of its mouth like a snake. 'Keep a distance, and let them speak for themselves.'

It hovered over the men and the boy, its feet scratching at the sand. 'You wanted to speak to Kassim, but he cannot answer. He is far from your speech. He is in the realm of Iblis, Lord of Jehannem.' The pale eyes glowed with a horrible amusement. 'He is not a lord there, let me assure you, oh kinsmen of Kassim.'

Shayk Abdullah opened his mouth, but no words came out. It was Husam who spoke, disdainfully. 'We know where Kassim is.'

'You know where Kassim is. Very well,' said the Grabber, and its wide jaws parted, in a horrible parody of a smile. 'Of course, it must be such a comfort to his kinsmen to know that he is amongst the damned of

Jehannem, and to know that he can never seek the pardon of the one he destroyed so treacherously, so no way is there to efface the curse through him. Now, ask your question.'

Soheila's heart burned with angry joy. That would tell them! Then she saw a shadow of triumph, quickly suppressed, pass over the faces of Husam and Abdullah, and knew that the ghoul had, without realising it, already answered one unspoken question. Reluctant admiration seized her again, though she tried hard to thrust it from her. She would never have had the guile and presence of mind to trick the ghoul and obtain extra information in the way Husam had, by a simple statement. She did not care to look too much at Khaled's face, his staring eyes and his extreme pallor. There could be no room for pity.

'You want to hear our question,' said Husam flatly.

'Yes!' shrieked the ghoul. 'Ask it, ask it! No, not you, Jinn-friend,' it growled, regarding Husam with sudden suspicion. 'One of the other ones, the kinsmen. They are the ones who should ask.' Its wicked eyes rolled, fixing on Khaled, who seemed to stagger and was only stopped from falling by Husam gripping his arm and supporting him.

Abdullah had gone very pale. But he moved forward, shielding Khaled from the ghoul's gaze with his body. His voice hardly trembled at all as he said, 'This then is my question: who among the Jinn can help the curse of Zohreh to be lifted from our house?'

The ghoul gave a sharp laugh. 'Could not your tame Jinn tell you? Only the Recorder of the Emerald Mountain of Kaf may annul such a curse permanently.'

'This is useless knowledge,' scoffed Kareen. 'Everyone knows that the Recorder of the Emerald Mountain of Kaf is one of the oldest and most powerful of all the Jinn, and records all the curses and wishes of mankind. But you know very well, Grabber, that she has rarely been known to annul a curse. And it is very difficult for a human to speak with her unscathed. So your answer is useless. It does not count. You have not answered the question at all.'

The ghoul's face twisted horrifyingly. 'You don't know anything, desert spirit!' it shrieked. 'I walk in the world of the dead, and I know such things have very occasionally happened. If a child of the house of Zohreh willingly gives the treasure of their house to a child of the house of Kassim, then there might be a chance. But still they will have to find the Emerald Mountain, and that is impossible, for they do not know how to find the way to it.' It hovered right in front of Abdullah, sending its stinking breath into his face. 'Now, I have answered that question. You likely have more. Come on, ask. Would you like to know how the Emerald Mountain may be reached?'

'We do not need to ask you,' cut in Kareen scornfully. 'I will find out.'

'You are wrong,' said the ghoul, shrieking with laughter now. 'It is a place only the dead, and those that walk with them, may go to unscathed.' It hovered closer. 'Come, ask me more! Oh, old man, come here and ask me a question, ask me the way, ask me the way. Ask me another question, ask me, for I crave sweet live flesh.' It loomed above them, its gaze fixed on Khaled, who fell to the ground. Husam and Abdullah immediately knelt beside him, shielding him with their bodies and their hands. Kareen leapt forward, placing herself between the ghoul and the humans. She lifted her head to the heavens and sang a single note – sweet, piercing and tuneful. And then it seemed to the terrified Soheila that a form, bright as noon, with great wings sprouting from its shoulders and a face so beautiful it could hardly be described, suddenly stood beside the Jinn.

'Back, Grabber,' said Kareen in a stentorian voice, 'back, in the name of He who made all. Back! You will not trap these humans into asking you a forbidden second question. These are not your rightful prey, and you have no call on them, as you well know. The Shining Ones are at my side, so you must fall back, Grabber, back into the darkness where you belong.' And she began to sing again. Her song was taken up by another deep, sweet voice, producing a music of such ravishing, warm, thrilling intensity that it made Soheila, frozen with awe and terror on her branch, feel the life rushing back redly into her veins.

The ghoul gave one bloodcurdling howl and vanished, as if the sand had swallowed it. Kareen, still singing, gestured to the men to move back towards the gate. As they reached it, Soheila saw Kareen incline her head towards the shining form at her side, once, twice, three times. She did not wait to see more. Her heart pounding, she climbed swiftly down the tree and ran, head down, dodging behind the low dunes, until she emerged, not far from the car. She could see the driver had come out and was standing with his back to her, looking at the gate in the mud wall. Now or never! She ran out from the shelter of the dunes, and was just about to reach the car when Abdullah, Husam, Khaled and Kareen emerged from the cemetery. The men, preoccupied with Khaled, who appeared deeply distressed, did not notice Soheila.

But Kareen saw her at once. In one bound, it seemed, the Jinn was on her, rolling with her on the sand, then hauling her up by the scruff of the neck.

'Little sneak! What are you doing here?' hissed Kareen, dangerously low, her glowing eyes fixed on Soheila's blue ones. Soheila could smell the Jinn's peculiar scent – like hot iron – and her heart nearly failed her, but she managed to say, low and unsteady, 'Nothing. I was just resting – sleeping – near the car – I saw you coming back and I thought I'd better get back in.'

Kareen took no notice of these protests, and dragged her back to Husam, Abdullah and Khaled.

They stared, astonished, at the kitchen boy dangling from Kareen's hand. 'What on earth —' began Husam. 'Payem, what are you doing here?'

Soheila was about to say something when Khaled raised his head and looked at her. There was something in his eyes that troubled her, something she didn't quite understand. It suddenly made her feel uncertain, and for one baffling moment, she wished she could tell him everything. Then the moment passed and she hardened her heart again. 'I must be careful,' she thought. 'I must be careful. He will be suspicious of me.'

Kareen shook her, none too gently. 'He stowed away, didn't you, little thief?'

'I am not a thief,' said Payem, looking away from Khaled's intense gaze. 'I — I — just wanted to feel what it was like to ride in a car like this — I've always dreamt —'

'This is the boy I told you about, who got us passage on the *Eagle* to come across the gulf,' said Husam to Abdullah. Turning to Payem, he said, 'So I presume you did get a job as a kitchen boy, child?'

Every moment, Soheila was expecting Khaled to say that she'd been snooping in the library, and had hidden behind the curtain when they came in, and heard what Bikaj had said. But he said nothing. Only once, his gaze fell on her again, then he whispered, 'I'll just go and sit in the car, Father. No, I am fine now, Father. I'd just like to go and sit down.' He walked a little unsteadily away from them, got in the car and shut the door. Soheila felt the slam of it like a reproach, though she had no idea why.

Kareen wasn't finished with her. 'What did you see, little sneak?'

'Nothing – nothing –' stammered Payem. 'I saw you go into the cemetery but why would I want to follow? I am scared of such places.' He gave a most convincing shudder, and fell on his knees before Abdullah. 'Forgive me, my lord. It was wrong and wicked of me to do this, but I only meant to see what it was like in the car. I do love these cars, sir. I thought you were just going for a nice drive in the desert. But I don't like cemeteries, they frighten me half to death. I just stayed by the car here, and rested.'

'I think it's unlikely the child watched,' said Abdullah. 'I do not think he would have been able to keep silent or unmoving in the face of the – what was in there – unless he has extraordinary powers for a boy of his age. You saw what it did to Khaled.'

'Still,' said Kareen, 'it would be best if you dismissed this boy from your employ at once. I don't like sneaks.'

'Oh, please, no sir, have mercy, please.' Payem threw himself before Abdullah. Tears filled his eyes. 'I have nothing – no-one – I was foolish – but I promise, sir, I promise I will never do it again. Please give me another chance.'

There was a tense silence. Then Abdullah shook his

head. 'I do not like to take bread from the mouths of needy children,' he said. 'Payem,' he went on, 'get up. Look at me.' The child did so. 'You should not have come with us without permission. It was very wrong of you.'

'I know, sir,' said Payem, eyes still swimming with tears. 'I am very sorry, sir. It won't happen again.'

'Perhaps you shouldn't be working in the kitchens, but in the garages,' said Abdullah, a little sharply, his eyes searching Payem's face.

Hardly daring to breathe, Payem said, 'I – I like working in the kitchens, sir. It's just that I've not seen cars as big as this before. We don't have ones like this where I come from. I could not help it.'

Abdullah smiled suddenly. 'Very well, Payem. Let's stop worrying about this, eh?' He turned to Husam and Kareen. 'Surely we have more to think about than castigating a silly, innocent child for liking cars too much.' He beckoned to Omar, who was standing some distance away. 'Have the goodness to inform whoever one should inform that this child was asked to come with us, to serve our food. I do not wish him to be in trouble in the kitchens.'

'Very good, sir,' said Omar, not seeming surprised by his master's request. But Soheila was not only surprised; she was also dismayed and disturbed. Nothing was as she had expected. She felt a great confusion of mind and heart. Why couldn't things be simple? Why couldn't there have been even more reason to hate the al-Farouks? Why couldn't they have been unkind or even cruel to her? Then she could have felt no doubt at all. She was afraid of the confusion that raced through her mind now, afraid of what it might mean. On the long weary journey to the palace she sat huddled in the back of the car, mind whirling, stomach churning, not daring to say a word or hardly make a move, under the suspicious scrutiny of the Jinn, who kept throwing glares at her from the rear-vision mirror. But Khaled never looked at her during the whole trip, and Soheila found that disturbed her almost as much as the Jinn's scrutiny.

Fifteen

All that afternoon and evening, Soheila worked hard in the kitchens, trying to numb herself. She could not allow herself to become weak just because the al-Farouks had showed kindness to her. She must take care to keep out of their way lest she falter in her task. She must not think of how terrible it was that she had to act treacherously, in secret. She had to remember that the al-Farouk ease and kindness were built on the bones and blood of her ancestor. She had to remember Kassim's guilt and the way, unacknowledged and unpunished, it had gone down the generations so that even that kind old man and his son were responsible, somehow. She had to remember that an avenger must harden her heart, must banish from it all human softness and uncertainty.

But revenge was no longer an abstract thing to her. She could picture it now, in horrid detail: herself, knife in hand, creeping up on the kind, crippled old Shayk or on gentle, handsome Khaled as they lay in their beds. She could imagine the red blood running, the betrayed look on their faces as they recognised their attacker. It was a horrible picture to her, though she most earnestly did not want it to be. She had spent so much of her life hating this family; she had spent so much of her life wishing to take revenge for the memory of her wronged ancestor. And yet here she was now like a soft fool, heartsick because of a picture in her mind, a picture of something she hadn't even done yet. 'Maybe,' she thought, 'I needn't kill them, only harm them greatly in some way.' But it seemed unlikely that would be Zohreh's wish. The ghost of her ancestor wanted blood for blood. It had to be done. How, she wasn't sure. She had to wait for the ghost to tell her. She would have to get back into the library tonight and try again to speak to it. But the thought made her shudder deep inside.

As she worked in the kitchen, the beginnings of an answer to her painful dilemma started to come to her. Maybe the way to harm the family was to find out what Zohreh's curse was exactly, and manouevre it so that it would come true. Then it would not be her but fate – Zohreh's curse – that would destroy them, and she would be free of this oppressive sense of guilt and shame.

She needed inside information, not from staff, but from within the centre of the house itself. She had to somehow pacify Khaled's doubts about her, perhaps even persuade him that she was a friend. He had been interested in the fact she might be an Akamenian; he might think she had information for him. She would pretend she did, and that way find out how the curse was to operate. Then she would watch and listen, and see if she could help it along. The thought cheered her up considerably. It made her feel as if she was doing something towards her mission, and less as if she was an abject failure, unworthy of Zohreh's memory, quailing in front of those burning, forceful eyes. Yes! She could face Zohreh's ghost tonight, fortified by her new resolution.

Kareen Amar was restless and anxious. Time was running out. She could feel the threat gathering. She could sense Zohreh's presence in the palace, getting stronger by the hour, though she could not see her. The ghoul was right. Only a few Jinns, and mostly wicked ones, have contact with the dead, for the cold world of shadows douses the living fire that is their essence. Nevertheless, she could feel the Akamenian's ghostly presence, and it worried her. Kareen was not at all sure she would be able to face an encounter with Zohreh's ghost but she must plan for it. She must get help from a Jinn who did have contact with the dead. And of course it must not be from a ghoul.

She spoke at length to Hamarajol and Farasha – knowing it would be no good trying to pull rank on

Bikaj again – and at last got a name: Ebon Zarah, the Jinn of the Skyflower Fountain, an oasis many hours south of Jumana, on the Riyaldaw road. According to the House-Jinns, Ebon Zarah was a good Jinn who had a great deal of deep power: he often spoke with the dead and he had encountered the most mysterious Jinn of all, the Recorder of the Emerald Mountain of Kaf.

The source of the al-Farouks' thorny problem lay within the world of the dead: Zohreh and Kassim. In Jehannem Kassim might well be – and she had no intention of visiting him there – but nobody had said which province of the afterlife Zohreh had gone to. The Jinn of the fountain might know. Anyway, it was worth a try. Kareen could not bear to sit jabbering with Husam and Abdullah, endlessly rehashing the ghoul's taunting words in the cemetery; or sifting through mountains of books in the library, searching for the Talisman and the answer to Bikaj's riddle; or trying to comfort Khaled, who as the hours wore on, was becoming more and more paralysed by fear and a sense of helplessness. She would set out at once, without telling anyone where she was going, for she had no idea if Ebon Zarah would prove to be of any use at all and she did not want to get anyone's hopes up in vain. Anyway, it was night, and likely she'd be back long before anyone had even realised she had gone.

Sixteen

Khaled lay unmoving on his bed. Shadows gathered in the corners of his room, but still he did not turn the light on. He was heartsick, not only with the gathering fear of what might happen in just two days' time, but because he had been profoundly shaken by the experience at the cemetery. It was partly the horror of being confronted by the evil, unclean ghoul that had affected him. Even more so, it was the realisation that his ancestor had been a man so wicked that only ghouls frequented the resting place of his bones: a man so evil that he'd been damned to the eternal fire of Iblis's realm. Though Khaled had known that with his mind before, now he knew it with his heart and his spirit, and that was much worse. So dispirited did he feel that he almost wished he had not tried to undo the curse; he felt almost as if he deserved it, merely because Kassim was his ancestor. If only he could have found Zohreh's family! If only he could have begun to undo the wrong that was done. 'Dear God in Heaven,' he prayed, 'please, bring peace to our sad world, preserve us from the evil of evil men, and the evil that lives after them.'

The other thing that troubled him was the presence of Payem at the cemetery. The boy had strange eyes – full of light, yet also with a curious blankness. A little shiver rippled over his skin. Payem had been hiding behind the curtain in the library when Bikaj had spoken of the graveyard; it must be why he had known to follow them there. But why had he? And why had he been looking at that book on the Akamenians?

Another shiver rippled over Khaled. He should tell his father and Husam and Kareen about it, but he couldn't bring himself to, remembering the light in the boy's eyes, his thin face, his frail body in its shabby clothes. Kareen already hated the boy; why make things worse for him? Perhaps he should try and talk to the child, directly, on his own, try and find out – gently, kindly – what it was that the boy sought. The thought made him feel much better, and he relaxed enough to drop into a light, fitful sleep.

In the library, Sharib worked busily away into the night with the clerks. He'd pointed his tame Jinns at this or that book, trying to find a shortcut to the question of just who Albalhol was, without success. Until, at last, just before midnight, the Jinn of the Glasses had lighted on a thin little book that had fallen behind one of the shelves. This cheap booklet — half-eaten by starving silverfish, for it had been overlooked by General Bikaj's platoons — was a souvenir from a trip someone in the family had taken long ago to the Royal Tombs at Teban, a remote site in the ancient country of Faraona, across the Narrow Sea. Reading what was left of the book, they discovered that Albalhol was a legendary monster from those remote parts: a monster with a snake's head, a lion's body and an eagle's wings who, so the story had it, lay in wait for unwary travellers on the road. Grabbing them in its huge paws, it asked them a riddle; and if they couldn't answer, it crushed them to death then ate them. Albalhol had in the end been defeated by a young magician-prince who had not only answered the riddle correctly, but had turned the monster to stone. The stone monster was still to be seen in those parts; the bad photograph accompanying the story in the booklet showed a huge statue in rather poor repair, with one of its wings half broken off.

Well, that discovery had caused a lot of excitement, with Husam and Abdullah summoned to share in it. As Albalhol was a creature of legend, surely the phrase 'in the arms of riddling Albalhol' was some kind of proverb or saying, they decided. Finding out its meaning should therefore point them in the right direction. Alas! There was no mention made of any such saying in what was left of the book. And because Teban was such an obscure place, there was nothing about the legend of Albalhol in any other book. Husam suggested that 'the arms of riddling Albalhol' might mean being in great danger, or perhaps even deliberately placing yourself in great danger. That seemed to have the ring of truth to it, but it did not greatly help them. Still, at least they had a lead now; they would concentrate tomorrow on books about Faraona, its culture, history and legends. No more work would be done that night. Everyone was too tired, the clerks' eyes red-rimmed with exhaustion, and even bouncy Sharib drooping a little. Rest, and night, might bring better counsel.

In her long wanderings through the human world in search of new songs Kareen Amar had almost forgotten how pleasant the company of her fellow Jinns could be. She liked her life, mostly, and her human friends a great deal, but the fact remained that sometimes she felt very much like a stranger – an immortal in the world of mortals, an elemental creature of power in the limited, but cosy, world of the Clay People. Yet she did not seek out the company of fellow Jinns. The wandering ones like herself were just as fiercely independent as she, the settled tribes or clans too haughty or provincial.

But the Jinn Ebon Zarah was a different sort of creature, neither lone wanderer nor jealous clansman. He was the spirit of the oasis known as the Fountain of the Skyflowers, which, because it was irrigated by underground springs, was unusually lush. It was carpeted in green grass studded with star-shaped flowers the colour of a deep blue winter sky. Time seemed to stand still in this beautiful place, which radiated an air of utter peace and tranquillity.

Ebon Zarah manifested as a very handsome young man, tall, black-haired and golden-skinned, with almond-shaped, long-lashed eyes of the same blue as the flowers. He wore a graceful sky-blue robe, and over that a silk coat in a slightly darker shade of blue, edged with gold. Instead of a headcloth he wore a kind of cap made of living flowers and sweet-smelling herbs. He carried a lute, around the neck of which were twined flowers. Not only was he handsome — Jinn, too, can be susceptible to good looks, and Kareen was no exception — but he was charming, gentle and interested in music. Also, he was very interested in Kareen's stories, which was another point in his favour. Kareen found herself not asking him questions but instead recounting all her exploits as they walked amongst the date plantations and wild-flower and herb gardens of the oasis, and then amongst a flock of fat-tailed sheep and a gathering of haughty camels that stared at the two Jinns in wary curiosity as they went past. They stayed away from the human camps, where weary nomads rested after long stints in the desert, but saw little girls in bare feet gathering armfuls of the skyflowers, and little boys in knee-length tunics having wrestling competitions on the soft grass. It was a place of sheer, peaceful magic and Kareen could feel herself relaxing and slowing down as she walked and talked with Ebon Zarah. They even sang a couple of songs together, Ebon Zarah accompanying Kareen on his lute. Her restless anxiety left her completely.

So it was a considerable time before Kareen finally bethought herself of why she'd come. She told Ebon Zarah the whole story, and he listened to her as attentively as he'd listened to all her other tales. When she finished, he was silent for a little while, then said, 'I would like to help you directly but I cannot, for I am limited in time and space to this place, and to the tribes that frequent this oasis. Neither Zohreh nor Kassim are in my sphere of influence. But I will give you this advice: it is true that the Recorder of the Emerald Mountain of Kaf can annul this curse. There is no one way to go to the Emerald Mountain, for it is a place that exists out of time and space. The journey is different in each case; it depends on the person who made the curse or the wish. You must find the right path from Zohreh herself. It will not be easy, for she must want to help.'

'I was afraid of that,' said Kareen gloomily. 'I can feel her there, in the palace. Her presence grows stronger all the time. And it does not feel like a benign presence.'

'If that is so,' said Ebon Zarah, 'then she must be persuaded somehow to give up her revenge. The child Khaled is right: this kind of curse is most potent on a significant anniversary such as this one. The vengeful spirit will know it is likely her last big chance, and her potency will be at its most dangerous on the day of his birthday.'

'And that's the day after tomorrow.'

'Do you know at what time he was born, exactly? That does make a certain difference.'

'I'm not sure,' said Kareen, 'but I will find out.'

'The worst would be if his birth time was close to the time Zohreh pronounced her curse, a hundred years before.' Ebon Zarah put a hand up to his hair and gently pulled out a flower, held it for a moment, murmuring words over it, and passed it over to Kareen. 'Take this with you back to the palace. It must be a human being who speaks to the ghost of Zohreh, not you, Kareen. Wearing this flower in their hair, they will be protected from harm, at least until the flower fades. Take care, though: the calling out of the ghost must be done when the power of the protective flower is at its height, at precisely midnight tomorrow night. The power will only last for a short time after that, for then the flower will wither and die, and its protection die with it. The ghost must be persuaded within that time.'

'Should it be Khaled who speaks to Zohreh?'

'Yes. He will be the best person to do so, except for a member of Zohreh's family. And you tell me they are all vanished.'

'That appears to be so,' said Kareen.

'Remember: the link will be strongest of all tomorrow night, at midnight. Later than that, Zohreh's curse will have much more potency than the flower could ever protect against.'

'I will remember,' said Kareen Amar, getting up.

'You do not need to go yet, Kareen Amar,' said Ebon Zarah, smiling enticingly up at her. 'It is a long time till tomorrow midnight, and the flower will last better here than outside. Stay with me a little longer, and teach me some of your songs. Your friend Khaled will be quite safe for the time being. Zohreh cannot strike yet.'

'Well —' said Kareen hesitantly, 'I am not sure that I —'

'I will tell you when it is time you must go,' said Ebon Zarah gently. 'You will be more useful to your friends if you are truly rested; your powers will be all the stronger. Being here, in this place where the living and the dead congregate in peace and safety, will give you strength to face the ghost, too, if it becomes absolutely necessary for you to do so. I promise you that, on my honour as a Jinn who can speak with the dead.'

'You are very persuasive,' said Kareen Amar, sitting down again with a sigh. Truth to tell, she was very glad to stay here a while longer, in the company of this charming and intriguing Jinn.

In the silent palace library, many miles away, Soheila stared into the carved mirror again, holding her ancestor's ashes.

'Zohreh, honoured one,' she murmured, 'will you grace me with your presence?'

The mirror stayed clear, but the air began to feel freezing cold again. Soheila's heart beat fast, and painfully.

'Grandmother of Grandmothers,' she whispered, 'please don't be angry with me. Please tell me what I must do.'

Suddenly the figure appeared in the mirror, unhooded, the ghastliness of it somehow diminished. Was it Soheila's imagination, or was the thing gaining more solidity, more form? Or perhaps she had become more used to the sight? But no, the face seemed less shapeless, and now there were lips, opening and closing on silent words. And the eyes – the eyes – they were more intense than ever, full of burning hatred, of rage, and of something else, something that looked rather like despair. The recognition of that suddenly made Soheila feel less afraid. A great tenderness flooded over her.

'Oh, Grandmother Zohreh,' she whispered, 'do not be sad. Justice will be done. I promise you that. I will not abandon you, ever.'

It seemed to her then that the cold in the room lessened. And all at once, in her mind came a murmured word. Just one: 'Talisman'.

'Must I do that first?' she asked the ghost in the mirror. 'Must I find the Talisman?'

Slowly, the figure nodded. Soheila's heart leapt. She said, 'Please, tell me more. How will I find it? And what should I do with it when I have it?'

'Talisman,' said the voice again, insistently in her head. Soheila stared into the mirror. 'But I do not know where it is. They have been looking for it, the al-Farouks, and they have not found it either. Don't you know where it is?'

The figure shook its head, very sadly. Soheila stood for a moment in thought. 'I should use them to find it. I must find out what they have discovered.' She looked into the mirror again. 'Is that right?'

But the figure of Zohreh had vanished. The mirror was clear once more. Soheila was alone.

Seventeen

Just before breakfast the next morning, Husam cracked the riddle of Albalhol. Or at least, he did so with the inadvertent help of Lotfi, a young Faraonan baker who had come to deliver fresh bread to the kitchens. The old swordsman had been on an early-morning stroll in the gardens, trying hard to think his way through the riddle, when Lotfi came whistling cheerfully in through one of the side gates, carrying a basket of new-baked bread that smelt very good indeed. He hailed Husam in a friendly manner. 'Up early, friend?'

'Couldn't sleep well,' Husam agreed. 'Head rather sore.'

'In the arms of riddling Albalhol, eh?' laughed Lotfi. Husam was about to say something vague and noncommittal when suddenly the full import of what Lotfi had said struck him. 'What did you say?'

Lotfi looked puzzled. 'An old saying from my village, friend, that's all.'

'But what does it mean?' said Husam excitedly.

Lotfi looked even more puzzled. 'It means to feel like you've got a cracking headache. Like when you have a hangover. It comes from a legend – the monster Albalhol, who used to like telling head-breaking riddles, and who would then crush his victims to death when they couldn't answer.'

'Light save us, it was Bikaj's little joke,' said Husam, staring at Lotfi; then without another word, he walked swiftly away, leaving an extremely puzzled Lotfi to shake his head over the strangeness of some people.

In the library, Husam, Abdullah and Khaled waited silently as Sharib adjusted his tame Jinn. Khaled's heart was beating fast; for the first time in hours, hope was rising in him again. Perhaps there might yet be time to forestall Zohreh's curse, once they had the Talisman.

'Jinn of the Glasses,' shouted Sharib at last, 'you must find the books here which are real head-breakers, so that those who read them feel as if they are in the arms of riddling Albalhol. Find me those books at once!'

'Oh Master, I hear and obey,' said the voice of the far-seeing Jinn. The glasses on Sharib's nose hopped up and down twice. The lenses shimmered and shook, and then resolved into rather blinding optical patterns, swirling round and round, colours changing. This went on for a few seconds, then gradually the glasses stilled, and the lenses stopped changing colour and became reflective. The voice of the Jinn said, 'Master, there are two such books in this place.'

'Very well,' said Sharib, as the others held their breath. 'Take me to them.'

The lenses revolved once; beams of light shot from them; and Sharib walked to the spot where the light was focused, on one of the bookshelves. He pulled out two slim books: one was in Parsarian, the other in Aksaran. Ceremoniously, he handed them to Khaled.

'This is a volume of poetry called *Songs of the Wanderer*,' said Khaled, opening the Aksaran book. 'Why would this be the right thing?'

'It's by a famous poet — it's said that he must have been frequently drunk, or a devotee of kalfkat,' said his father a little uncomfortably. 'The poems don't always make sense, you see.'

'Perhaps the Talisman is hidden in this,' said Khaled, excited. He flipped the book open and flapped the pages to see if anything fluttered out. But nothing did. He checked the thin binding and the paper jacket. Nothing. He took up the next book, which was a sermon against the use of kalfkat. Again he flapped at the pages, but nothing came out. This binding was thicker, the cover more sturdy — but there was nothing there.

'Oh dear,' said Husam, 'this appears to be another joke. Or perhaps a riddle, appropriately enough.'

Sharib had been standing with a pleased smile on his lips but now he came forward, frowning. 'There must be some kind of mistake,' he said. 'My Jinn was quite sure these books fit the description. You don't appear to have any books on wine or wine-growing in here, either, which might also fit, or collections of drinking songs.'

'Certainly not,' said Abdullah a little stiffly. 'I never drink, and neither does any of my household.'

'I don't understand,' said Sharib, scratching his head. Then the Jinn of the Glasses suddenly said in a high, piercing voice, 'Once there was another, but it is no longer here. And it is not in my power to tell you which or where.'

As it spoke, Bikaj suddenly appeared on the table before them. Ignoring the others, he addressed himself directly to Abdullah. 'Lord al-Farouk,' he said, 'we have always been the loyal servants of your family. We have kept insects from your books and rot from the knowledge of your family. Why then are we being punished by having rude foreign Jinns invade our precincts? First the red-head gypsy, and now this shallow modern creature hiding in the glass, who cannot even manifest into any respectable shape. It is intolerable, sir!'

Abdullah stared at Bikaj, his lips twitching a little. 'They are here under my authority,' he managed to say at last. 'You would not help us, Bikaj, so we were forced to consider other means.'

'I would have helped if I had been asked properly, by the master of this house,' said Bikaj with great dignity.

Abdullah put a weary hand to his head. Sharib said harshly, 'It is you who is a shallow creature, Jinn. You should know that the protection of your house means much more than pettifogging bossiness. Shame on you, playing silly games!'

'You should not speak to my great eldest brother like that,' squeaked an excited little voice; and in the next moment, Farasha appeared next to Bikaj, waving his six legs frantically. 'You're not an al-Farouk, to speak to him thus.'

Khaled intervened, choosing his words very carefully so as not to offend the touchy Jinns. 'But I am. And I'm asking you, dear Farasha, my helpful friend, and General Bikaj, who commands such great platoons, please, lay aside your justified anger, and help us.'

'General Bikaj,' chimed in Abdullah, 'would you be so good as to tell your master, me, Shayk Abdullah al-Farouk, where we might find the book that lies in the arms of riddling Albalhol, the book where is hidden the Talisman of the Star? I am mindful of the great service your platoons have rendered my family over the decades, but I ask you also to be mindful of the need for the continued existence of the al-Farouks. And that might not be assured if you do not answer truthfully; then, General Bikaj, where would you and your platoons be?'

The Library-Jinn looked up at him with its goggling eyes, waved a feeler and said haughtily, 'We will always serve the al-Farouks, if we are asked properly. That is all we ask. The book you seek is not in my domain; it is in Farasha's. In the domain of discarded books.'

'What? What?' squeaked Farasha. Immediately he drew himself up, and a look of ineffable pride came over his silly features. 'Of course. I will show it to you! Come, come, come with me.' And he flew up into the air in great agitation, his ragged wings beating jerkily. 'Come! There is no time to lose.'

'So you know which book it is, Farasha, do you?' said Sharib, making as if to grab the Jinn. 'Why didn't you tell us before?'

'Because he didn't know, of course,' said Bikaj with great scorn. 'He is only the youngest brother of our clan, in charge of an unimportant domain. He does not need to know such things.'

'Well then, brother Bikaj, time to tell us exactly which book it is,' said Sharib with a coarse laugh, as Farasha drooped a little. Bikaj turned his back on the Jinn master, very deliberately. 'I will not address you, rude personage,' he huffed. 'I will only address the master of the house.'

'Please tell us, dear General Bikaj,' said Shayk Abdullah. Bikaj sniffed, but seemed mollified. 'Very well. It is called *A Short Account of the Proceedings of the Royal Society into Research on the Greater and Lesser Species of Silverfish, 1900 Session*,' he intoned in a grand voice.

There was a moment's stunned silence, then a general burst of laughter.

'Well, well,' chuckled Sharib, 'I am sure it is of such thundering dullness you would indeed have to be in the arms of riddling Albalhol to even consider the folly of turning its pages.'

To everyone's amazement, Bikaj gave a tiny, wintry smile. 'It is indeed indigestible, even to silverfish,' he allowed. 'Which is why it has sat safely in Farasha's domain for years and years. It is in that book you will find what you seek. And well rid will we be of the thing it hides, for it does not belong to this house.' He bowed once to Abdullah, once to Khaled, then with a clap of pages snapping together he vanished.

'Now, now, come with me,' squeaked Farasha. 'I will guide you to my domain. Come with me.' And happily unaware of the fact that nobody needed his guidance to go to the storeroom, he flapped jerkily up and away, beside himself with excitement.

Soheila had been sent to empty out a pail of slops into the compost bins in one of the yards. She had just done it when she heard a voice she recognised as Khaled's, floating from the open window of a room that backed onto the yard. She crept closer to listen. He sounded excited. 'Here it is, Father, here it is!' Then she heard the others' voices raised in joyful unison. Her heart leapt in her chest. She must see what they had.

She looked around wildly for something to stand on. The bucket! It was a big steel bucket, strong enough to hold her light weight. She up-ended it, got on top and stood on tiptoes to look through the small window. Khaled, his father, Husam and a dwarf were standing around in a circle in a dusty storeroom, gazing at something Khaled held in the palm of his hand. It was a beautiful, carved white wooden box that seemed to shine with a soft, otherworldly radiance. Soheila's blood pounded in her head. She didn't need the voice of Zohreh to tell her that this was her family's lost treasure, the Talisman of the Star.

'We will have to keep it safe,' she heard Abdullah say.

'I can keep it in my room,' Khaled answered. Soheila clenched her fists. It wouldn't stay there long, she thought fiercely. Somehow, she'd contrive a way to get into Khaled's room tonight and take back what was rightfully hers. For now, though, she'd better get back to the kitchens before Miss Josephine missed the kitchen boy Payem and sent someone out to look for him. Slipping down from her bucket and hurrying back to the kitchen, she did not notice Farasha, who, hovering happily above the door of his domain at the spot where he intended to have them write up a really wonderful, sonorous formula in his honour, happened to catch a glimpse of her creeping away. Farasha was far too happy to care about what a ragged kitchen boy might be doing skulking around looking through windows, and so he did not say anything to anyone about it but fluttered down amongst his delighted human friends, adding his thin, squeaky voice to their conversation.

If anyone had been standing in that spot just a few minutes later they might have seen a disturbing sight. A man was peering over the high wall of the yard. He had a handsome but cruel face and was clean-shaven, with very black, smooth hair, and cold, hungry eyes of a curious amber colour, with yellow lights in them. He looked this way and that, as if assessing something, then, just as suddenly as he had appeared, vanished again.

Eighteen

The Talisman of the Star sat quietly in its box on the table, keeping its secrets to itself. Khaled could hardly believe it was there at all. It was strange to think that the person who had last handled it had been Kassim; and presumably, just before him, Zohreh. And long before her, Melkior.

It made him feel better just knowing they had found it. There was something emanating from it – something good, even beautiful, that seemed to enter into his very bones. He was no longer oppressed by the knowledge of Kassim; his heart was stronger now, and he felt less afraid. They had under a day now to break the curse, but all at once he was sure they would do it. It would happen. No-one before had found the Talisman. It seemed a very good sign indeed.

Sharib had pointed the Jinn of the Glasses at the carved box and received in reply the information that the box was made from the wood of the starbranch tree, a small, very rare native Parsarian tree that only grew on a certain hillside north of Shideh. The wood had been carved, the Jinn said, by a master craftsman in the employ of Melkior, the Magvanda of the Stars, many hundreds of years before. But when Sharib had attempted to get the Jinn to focus on the coil of fabric inside the box, it had shrieked, 'That cannot be! Cannot be! It has been touched by one of the Shining Ones, and so it is not in my power to give you any information about it. Only the heir to the house of Melkior can do that. Do not ask me again, Master. It is forbidden for me to say any more about it.' Then it had refused to say another word.

They guessed that the thin, faded strip of fabric might have been part of the clothing of the baby prince whom Melkior and his students had gone to pay homage to. What its powers were they had no idea, and no way of finding out. Except for...

'What about Kareen?' said Abdullah. 'She knows many things, has wandered many places, and we saw a Shining One by her side at the graveyard, did we not? She is a powerful spirit; she may be allowed to say more than a minor Jinn.'

'Where *is* Kareen?' said Husam, frowning. 'Has anyone seen her lately?'

They realised suddenly that no-one had seen her since the evening before.

'Kareen always does her own thing,' said Husam,

sighing. 'She is off on some hunt of her own, I'll be bound.'

'Probably another flying carpet,' said Khaled, laughing.

'Or some other contraption,' agreed Abdullah, pleased to see his son looking so well and cheerful.

'Can you try and get your bloodhound to track her down?' said Husam to Sharib, who shook his head.

'No, not other Jinn,' he said. 'We cannot track anything to do with the wild free ones – my goodness!' he exclaimed. 'Speak of the Jinn, and she shows her fiery face.'

Kareen Amar had just walked into the room, looking, indeed, rather hot and bothered. As soon as she came in, she saw the Talisman on the table. She gave a little cry. 'You have found it!'

'But what does it do, Kareen? Do you know? Can you tell us?'

Kareen looked at the box. She made no attempt to touch it. She said quietly, 'It is not a thing of power, but a token of love and gratitude. It is a thing without price, beyond value. It is the treasure of the house of Melkior.'

'The treasure of the house of Melkior,' they all echoed.

Khaled said, 'I would be so happy if I could do what is needed to break the curse and lay the spirit of Zohreh to rest. If only a son or daughter of her house were here, we could beg them to –'

'Don't be foolish, my son,' said Abdullah heavily. 'Not only is there no child of the house of Zohreh here, but why would such a one want to give us the treasure of their house, which our ancestor already stole from them?'

No-one spoke for a little while, for who could give a positive answer to such a question?

Then Abdullah got up and said decisively, 'I will go and see the Prince at once and ask him to send an urgent message directly to the top of the Government of Parsari. We must find the Melkior family.'

'An excellent notion,' said Kareen Amar. 'It must be done. I will stay here with Khaled and keep him safe.'

'I will come with you, too, sir,' said Sharib. 'I wish to tell the Prince what happened to Mr Harir, the carpet dealer.'

'Very well,' said Abdullah. 'We will go there now and be back very soon.'

'I will stay with Kareen and Khaled,' said Husam. 'My sword will be at their service.'

Kareen nodded. 'And we must put the Talisman in a safe place. I suggest the library, under the direct care of Bikaj. If he is bound by a written request from you, Shayk, he will protect it completely.'

'Very well,' said Abdullah, getting up and going to his desk. He scribbled something on a piece of letterhead, signed it and imprinted it with the seal on his ring. 'Now, Khaled, please do whatever Kareen and Husam tell you to. Promise me.'

'Yes, Father,' said Khaled.

When the others had left, Husam turned to Kareen. 'Where were you?'

'Visiting a new friend,' said Kareen. And she told them an edited version of her visit to Ebon Zarah's oasis. She ended by saying, 'So at what time were you born, Khaled?'

'At about eight o'clock in the morning.'

'Very well. You should be safe enough till eight tomorrow morning. That leaves us time to summon Zohreh's ghost tonight. Now we have found the Talisman, too, we may be able to lay her to rest.'

Husam said, 'We should take it to the library now and put it in Bikaj's care.'

Khaled gingerly picked up the box. He touched the delicate carved tracery. Was it perhaps just a trifle warm to the touch? Or was that his own warmth, holding it, and his imagination supplying the rest?

'I wish we knew where Zohreh's family was,' he whispered. 'This is theirs. It should be with them, for Kassim stole the treasure of their house, as well as their ancestor's life.'

'If you're so keen on giving it to them,' Kareen said, 'you might well be able to hand it to Zohreh herself when we summon her tonight.'

Husam and Khaled looked at each other, the same

thought going through their heads. Kareen seemed very sure of herself, but did the Jinn really know how the ghost would react? Khaled gave a little shiver, quickly repressed. He must concentrate on the positive things, must not allow terror to paralyse him as it had done last night, or he was done for.

Nineteen

Payem made a lot of mistakes that morning in his work and his ears soon rang from the heavy hand of Miss Josephine. 'What's the matter with you, are you sickening for something?' yelled the exasperated second cook, at last, when Payem dropped a couple of eggs on the floor. 'If you are, I'd rather you were out of the kitchen, we don't want everyone coming down with whatever you've got.' She peered critically into the child's face. 'Your eyes are bloodshot, and you're flushed.' She put a hand to Payem's forehead. 'Yes, you're definitely sickening for something, probably some kind of fever, by the feel of you. Be off with you to the dormitory. Best thing for fever is to go to bed and sleep it off. If you get worse we'll get the healer sent in. Go on, off you go,' she went on, crossly, when Payem tried to stammer thanks, 'no point in having a sick boy cluttering up the place!'

Soheila didn't really feel sick; she was just exhausted, in mind and body. She hadn't meant to mess up in her work, because she didn't really want any extra attention being paid to her, but now she felt that an undreamt-of opportunity had come her way, and she must use it.

So instead of heading for the dormitory, she prowled along the corridors, her footsteps irresistibly leading her back to the library. Though she wanted to get the Talisman from Khaled's room, where she thought it had been hidden, it was not easy to get into the family's private quarters, and besides, she needed to speak to Zohreh again. As she approached the door, she heard the sound of voices within, and flattened herself into a niche in the corridor. No sooner had she done so than the library door opened and Khaled, Husam and the red-headed Jinn came out, talking softly to each other. She strained her ears to hear what they were saying, but only caught the odd word here and there, '. . . Talisman . . .', '. . . tonight . . .', '. . . careful . . .', 'Zohreh's family . . .', '. . . once and for all . . .' It was enough to make her tremble, from fright and anger. Her mind whirled with suppositions. Were they going to try to use the Talisman to efface the curse? Maybe they thought they could use it to find the rest of Zohreh's family and finally exterminate them all? And they were going to do it tonight. Her heart burnt anew at their wickedness. She would stop them. No more mercy, no more wishy-washy silliness, she must accomplish her ancestor's curse, whatever it was.

She waited until they had walked down the corridor and were out of sight, then slipped into the library.

She went straight to the mirror. 'Grandmother of Grandmothers,' she whispered, 'please show yourself to me. Please speak to me.'

She looked into the mirror. It only reflected her own face. She whispered, 'They have found the Talisman, Grandmother of Grandmothers. They have found the treasure of our house.'

Zohreh's figure appeared suddenly in the mirror. Her outline was much sharper now, her features almost human, but her eyes as burning as ever. She heard her ancestor's voice in her head. 'Today. It must be today.'

'But Grandmother Zohreh —'

'Tomorrow he is fifteen. Tomorrow, he thinks is the day. But it was today,' said the voice, very clearly now. 'He made a mistake in his counting. He forgot a leap year. Today, a hundred years ago, I died at the hands of a murderer. Today is when my curse will be most potent of all. But I need your help, Soheila, to accomplish it most perfectly. You must not fail me.'

Soheila stammered, 'But I —'

Zohreh said, quietly, 'My child, you are here, in the house of our enemies. In the house that saw my blood spurt red on the floor. Will you deny me now?'

Soheila gulped. She whispered, 'Please, tell me, how may I do it? Tell me, what is the instrument of your curse?'

'Fire, burning fire,' came Zohreh's voice in her head.

'How must it be done?' Soheila's voice shook,

though she tried to control it. Surely Zohreh did not wish her to set fire to the palace or to burn Khaled alive?

The ghost's next words both baffled and relieved her. 'In one hour, go to the back garden. One hour, you understand?'

'In one hour, I must go to the back garden,' repeated Soheila slowly. 'But why? What should I do there?'

'Go to the back garden,' said Zohreh. 'That is all you need to know. You must do it, for you are bound to your promise to me. Justice must be done.'

And she, was gone. Soheila was left standing there, trembling violently. She wanted to ask more questions – she wanted to run away. She wanted to do what Zohreh said she must do – she wanted to run to Khaled and warn him to be careful, not to go near any fires. She berated herself for her weakness, and forced herself to remember Kassim's merciless murder of her ancestor. She must do it. Blood for blood.

She racked her brains, trying desperately to think how the curse might strike Khaled through her going into the garden. There was no fire out there – but perhaps it would be some other thing, like a bolt of lightning hitting him? Yet it was a perfect, cloudless day, not a sign of storm. She dragged herself slowly back to her quarters and lay on her bed, watching the hands of the clock go round, thinking about the curse, wondering how many other deaths there might have been, imagining the terror and pain of dying by fire. It was horrible – horrible – but she was trapped. She was bound to her promise to Zohreh, and she could not back out.

The palace was quiet when she got up an hour later and slipped out. Khaled was in his room, reading, while Husam, his sword across his knees, dozed in a big arm-chair by Khaled's bed. Kareen prowled the corridors of the palace, talking to the House-Jinns, and the servants were all busy with their multifarious tasks. Nobody saw her.

She was in the garden now. It was quiet and still, and full of sunlight. She had no idea what to do. Slowly, she made her way to a stone bench and sat down. A fountain played near her but she hardly saw it or heard it. She did not even think of Zohreh, or try to summon her ghost. Her mind was full of fire. Roaring, red and yellow flames. She saw Khaled's bright, handsome face, his hand reached out to her in friendship. Then she saw his dark eyes wide with terror, in a ring of flame, his hands outstretched, pleading . . . pleading . . . Oh, Khaled, Khaled, her heart wept, how I wish . . . how I wish . . .

'Ugh!' she gave a strangled cry as someone's arm gripped her round the throat. She tumbled off the bench, kicking and struggling, trying to catch her breath to scream. A figure loomed over her: not a spy from the house, as she'd half suspected, but a stranger, dressed in blue jeans, a pale shirt and a leather jacket. Something bright swung at his neck. He had a black headcloth tied around the lower half of his face so only his eyes were visible. In that instant of utter terror, Soheila saw a cruel, hungry yellow glare: a glare that was not quite human.

She had time to utter one pitiful scream before the man pinned her down. She spat up at him, and he growled, deep in his throat, and drew a knife. 'Shut up. The al-Farouk boy. Where is he?'

Soheila's heart twisted. Her mind filled with Zohreh's words. This was how it was meant to happen. Part of her – the violent, vengeful part – wanted to say, 'Khaled? You want Khaled? I'll give you Khaled . . .' but the rest of her wouldn't let her. The words would not come, they would not leave her mind. Instead, she opened her mouth and gave a choked, desperate warning howl, quickly cut off by the man's stunning blow.

Khaled's room looked out onto the back garden. He had tried to read but he was restless and couldn't settle down, unlike Husam, who snored peacefully in his chair. He was pacing about when he heard the scream. In an instant he was at the window, looking into the garden, and saw Payem struggling with a veiled stranger, then saw the stranger hit the boy, hard, so that he crumpled to the ground. He didn't think twice, but jumped out of the window and threw himself on the man.

It was like throwing himself at a brick wall. He was stunned by the man's strength. It was all over quite quickly. A blow to the side of his head knocked him cold; in the next instant, he was gagged, trussed, and thrown over the man's shoulder. Then the man flung a rope ladder over the wall and swarmed up it with his burden. He reached the top of the wall and dropped down. Seconds later, a car started up, and roared away.

Soheila had come to just in time to see the man disappearing with Khaled over his shoulder. Her head ached and her heart hammered. What had happened? Why had Khaled come into the garden? Then full memory returned to her. She rocked back and forth on her haunches, moaning quietly, trying to think. He must have heard the struggle. He must have come out to help her. And so he had been kidnapped. Was this what Zohreh had wanted?

'No, no, no,' she whispered to herself, brokenly. 'This isn't right. It isn't right.' She gave an involuntary shudder as she remembered those cold, cruel eyes. Eyes with a cold fire burning in them. A cold fire. Oh God, oh Lord Akamenia, what would the man – or the thing – do to Khaled? No. She did not want this. She did not.

'Grand-daughter,' came Zohreh's voice in her head, suddenly, harshly, 'grand-daughter, this is not a time to be weak. You must get back the treasure of our family. You must put my spirit to rest.'

'Oh, Grandmother of Grandmothers,' wept Soheila, 'I am weak, and I do not know what to do any more.' She thought, 'I was the bait for poor Khaled. I trapped him. If I had not come out into the garden, he would not have been kidnapped, taken into the power of Yellow Eyes. What is he? Oh God, what is he?'

'Grand-daughter,' said Zohreh, very sharply indeed, 'that was no demon. It was a man – an enemy of this house.'

'But why did you make me –'

'You could not kill him yourself,' said Zohreh's voice coldly. 'It was best this way. The curse will be accomplished, as it should. He is the only child of this house. Now the house of al-Farouk will die, and justice will truly be done.'

'No!' shouted Soheila. She put her hands over her ears. 'I will not listen to any more. I will not!'

She broke off abruptly. She'd heard noises in Khaled's room, and a familiar voice calling out, 'Husam?' She panicked. The red-headed Jinn! She knew Kareen Amar did not like her, or trust her; she'd have no mercy if she discovered what had happened. Soheila would have to hide, and quickly.

Kareen Amar had spoken to a few of the House-Jinns, but hadn't learnt much. Down near the repository of forgotten books she came across Farasha, who was still fluttering in a state of great excitement over the sensational find in his own domain. He was inclined to keep jabbering at Kareen about it, and she was about to make her excuses and leave, when he said, 'The news of the great find is so wondrous that it has reached the ears of even the most insignificant kitchen boy!'

'A kitchen boy?' said Kareen. 'What do you mean? What did he look like?'

'Like a kitchen boy,' shrugged Farasha indifferently. 'A little greaser: scrawny, small, spiky black hair and round eyes like a wild kitten. Wore an apron.'

'Payem,' said Kareen. 'What did he do?'

'He just stood and stared through the window in awe,' said Farasha, modestly adding, 'Perhaps he saw me, too.'

Kareen frowned. Without a word to Farasha, she turned and went striding towards the kitchens, Farasha fluttering behind her in a rather indignant way. He'd only just begun to enjoy himself recounting his experiences; he wasn't about to let the other Jinn escape so easily.

The appearance of the odd foreigner in the palace kitchens caused a bit of a stir; the family rarely came into these precincts, and guests never. The staff were even more surprised to discover the weird redhead had come looking for the new kitchen boy. When Miss Josephine, with an undertone of incredulous contempt at the foreigner's bad manners, told Kareen briskly that she'd sent the boy to bed because he was sick, she was most miffed when the redhead turned abruptly and left without a word. It took Miss Josephine a minute or two, and the relief of boxing Ismail's ears for staring, to recover.

Meanwhile Kareen strode along to the servants' dormitory, Farasha following her. He hadn't gone into the kitchens, it being beneath his dignity as a Book-Jinn to go into such a place, but he was determined to see what Kareen was up to. He tried to speak to her, but she took no notice. When they reached the dormitory, which of course was empty, she stood there for a moment, then stalked off to the servants' bathroom, much to Farasha's disgust. He was even more disgusted when she called the Bathroom-Jinn's name. Hamarajol was of the lowest possible caste of House-Jinns; if Farasha associated with him publicly he would lose rank. Farasha could hardly believe that a powerful Jinn like Kareen Amar would stoop to speak to one as lowly as Hamarajol, and thought that a long sojourn in foreign parts must have effaced the Jinn's knowledge of what was seemly and what was not in Al Aksara. Or perhaps the free spirits were like that: unlike House-Jinns, they had no notion of the finer things in life.

Despite his indignant twitterings to himself, Farasha's curiosity still got the better of him. He had lived for a long time untroubled by questions or wonderings, and he hardly even realised that he had changed. He just knew he had to know, and that this feeling would not leave him alone. So he fluttered about anxiously at the door to the bathroom and finally settled in a rather gingerly fashion on the door-jamb, for thus it could be said he had not, properly speaking, entered the unclean domain. He hoped Hamarajol would have enough sense of propriety to pretend he wasn't there, but in this he was wrong.

'Ha, Farasha!' said Hamarajol, interrupting Kareen as she asked him if he knew where Payem was, 'come for a bit of slumming, have you, old friend? Well, well, wonders will never cease.'

'I am not your friend,' said Farasha, quite forgetting that one shouldn't answer impertinence from an inferior. 'And I am not slumming. I have come as the representative of House-Jinns, and command you to answer our honoured guest.'

Hamarajol gurgled with laughter, his yellow eyes in his shapeless grey body sparkling with mirth. 'Well, then, it seems I can do naught but answer, oh august Farasha.'

'I am glad to see you have at last come to your senses and seen what is seemly,' said Farasha – and goggled in a bewildered fashion at Hamarajol's and Kareen's amusement.

'Now then,' said Hamarajol, in a mock solemn tone, 'now that we have observed the formalities, and seeing as how I have none other but an exalted representative of the House-Jinns here in my humble abode, I will tell you both that I have precisely no idea where the child you are looking for is. However, if I were you, I should look in the garden. I have heard from my sources there – my old friend the Jinn of the compost heap, to be precise – Farasha, you'd love to meet him, must introduce you one of these days – that the person in question is always skulking in and out of there, probably avoiding work, but perhaps for nefarious purposes. Who knows, given the ways of the Clay People?'

'Thank you, Hamarajol, we will go and see if we can find the kitchen boy in the garden,' said Kareen. She was turning to leave when the yellow eyes twinkled and the Bathroom-Jinn said, in an elaborately casual voice, 'Of course, if you're looking for a suspicious kitchen *boy*, you might be looking for quite a while.'

'What do you mean?'

'Well,' said the Bathroom-Jinn, with a coarse laugh that made Farasha squirm, 'very little can be hidden here in my domain. Let's just say I have incontrovertible proof that your kitchen boy is no boy at all.'

'Payem is a *girl*?'

'Certainly seems like it,' said Hamarajol, and his grey blubbery mass shook with laughter.

'But why would the child dress up as a boy, just for a job in the kitchens? They employ girls there, too. It makes no sense.'

'Search me,' said Hamarajol lightly. 'Who knows what Clay People do things for?' He winked at Farasha. 'Well, best get on, my friends. I will treasure the memory of the day a Book-Jinn came to visit me. What tales I'll have to tell my friends in the compost heap, and the drains.'

'If you dare —' began Farasha, furiously, looking to Kareen Amar for support. But Kareen Amar was gone.

Twenty

Soheila crouched behind some bushes, wretched and sick. She should go and sound the alarm, she thought, but if she did they'd want to know why she'd tarried in telling them what had happened. 'They'll think I was in on it,' she thought. 'They'll beat me – punish me – maybe even kill me, who knows?' She could feel hot tears banked up inside her eyes, but refused to let them out. She tried to get a grip on herself, to harden her heart. She was a descendant of Zohreh, after all. She could not cry; she must not be weak. But her head ached horribly. She did not want Khaled to be hurt – yet she had had to do as Zohreh wanted. She tried to tell herself she hardly knew Khaled, so why should his fate upset her so? What was more, he was an al-Farouk; he was from a family who were enemies to her own.

But her mind kept returning to him, slung helplessly over Yellow Eyes's shoulder as if he were a sack, not a person. She could imagine his terror and pain all too well. She groaned inwardly.

Oof! The breath was knocked out of her suddenly. She found herself on the ground, staring up at two wild, furious faces: the red-headed Jinn with the old swordsman behind her.

'Who are you, really?' said Kareen Amar, and her eyes glowed dangerously. 'Don't you dare lie to me or I'll frizzle you in an instant.' A flame leapt from her fingers. 'Don't think I wouldn't, you little spy, you thief.'

Husam's face was stern and angry. 'Why have you come here? Tell us at once, or it'll be the worst for you.'

Terror instantly filled Soheila but she managed to say, 'My name is Payem, I'm a Parsarian —'

'I said no lies!' said the Jinn, grabbing Soheila by the scruff of her neck and pulling her to her feet. She loomed over the child, her breath as hot as the wind from the desert. 'Payem is a boy's name, and you're a girl.'

Something like a moth fluttered down from the low branch of a tree and landed on Kareen's shoulder. A petulant voice said, 'Don't deny it, girl. We know. The Bathroom-Jinn told us.'

Soheila stared for a moment at this new shock; then she swallowed, bent her head and, said softly, 'Very well. It is true. I am a girl. But I —' She swallowed again, and said in a voice thick with real tears, 'I am the oldest child of a widow in Shideh and my mother and twin baby sisters depend on my wages to survive. I thought that if I came on my own as a girl to Ameerat it might be difficult and even dangerous for me. So I dressed up as a boy. I did not intend any harm by it.'

Kareen Amar stared at her. 'You are not telling the truth.' Her eyes were narrow.

'We have just come from Khaled's room,' said Husam. 'He has vanished. Where is he?'

'How should I know?' cried Soheila, nearly mad with terror and shame and sorrow. 'How should I know? I am not his keeper.'

'I saw her!' shouted Farasha. His google eyes were popping out of his head. 'She was looking into my room. And she heard you talking about the Talisman. She's a spy. She's been sent to steal the Talisman, and take away young master.'

'No! No!' shouted Soheila.

'Just as I thought,' said Kareen with grim satisfaction. 'The al-Farouks have taken a snake to their bosom.' She shook Soheila like a rat, her long nails digging painfully into the child's flesh under the thin cloth of her tunic. 'You'd better start talking, girl, and fast.'

'Tell us. What did you want with the Talisman?' demanded Husam. 'Who sent you? What is your real name?'

Soheila looked into Husam's eyes, then Kareen Amar's, and saw no mercy there. She looked at

Farasha's excited pop-eyes and thought, bleakly, this is it, I'm going to die, just like my ancestor; I'm going to finish here in the palace of my enemies, frizzled to death by the wild fire of a Jinn, or run through by a swordsman's weapon; I'll never see home again, or my parents, or my brother.

A mixture of fury, pride, guilt and grief seized her then, and she shouted, 'I don't know the answer to your first questions. I have done nothing to Khaled and I do not know where the Talisman — my family's Talisman — is. You are the ones who have it. Know that my true name is Soheila of the Melkior clan, and I am the great-great-great-grand-daughter of the wonderful and courageous lady who was so foully and treacherously slain by the wicked murderer and thief Kassim al-Farouk. One of the last of my name and my religion and my family, I came to Ameerat to avenge the death of my ancestor, to bring death and dishonour and distress to the family of al-Farouk, as it was brought on the innocent Melkior clan. Put me to death if you must — but with my last breath I will fortify Zohreh's curse with such dark power that it will destroy everyone here, and bring these walls tumbling down.' She had straightened herself in Kareen's grasp; her head was flung back; her eyes shone with a ferocious intensity. She would die like a daughter of the house of Zohreh should, without fear. It was a moment before she realised the quality of the silence around her, and then she looked up to see that Kareen's grip had loosened, Husam looked completely stunned, and Farasha was frozen like a goggling statue on the Jinn's shoulder.

Kareen said, very quietly, 'You are a daughter of the house of Zohreh, truly?'

Soheila did not understand what was happening or why neither of them made any effort to kill her. She said harshly, 'I am not lying.'

'No,' said Husam coldly. 'We see that. But we see much more. We see that you disgrace the memory of your great and courageous ancestor, coming in like a masked thief into the house of trusting and kind people, prepared to weave evil plots in darkness, repaying kindness and hospitality with deceit and dissimulation.'

Hot tears sprang into Soheila's eyes. The words hurt, especially coming from Husam, who had championed her as Payem. 'You don't understand. My ancestor's spirit is here. I must do as she wants. Justice must be done.'

'And what do you call justice?' said Husam. 'A stab in the back perhaps, or, as you're a kitchen boy, a dose of cold poison, in secret? Or a match to their bedroom curtains? Ah, truly it is a wonder you think fit to claim ownership of the Talisman of the Star, which is a token of love and gratitude, not of ugly treachery and cold-blooded murder. Your family does not deserve it.'

Soheila's face flushed. Her heart was wrung with hatred and shame. She spat out, 'I will not listen to you, in the name of Akamenia, my Lord and my God, and his Truthteller, who protected against all evil spirits.'

'You are a little fool,' said Husam wearily, 'a little fool. Did you not realise that the al-Farouks have been sorry all down the long years for what Kassim did, and have tried to find your family?'

'Find us, yes,' said Soheila, eyes flashing, 'to finally destroy us!'

'You thick-headed idiot,' snapped Kareen, 'it was to find you and make reparations to you, much as you don't deserve it.'

'It is time this curse was ended,' said Husam. 'It is time Zohreh's spirit be put to rest. Don't you see? That is what we are here for, Kareen and I. That is what Khaled and the Shayk want: not only to be safe, but to see that justice is finally done, that your family is compensated for the loss of its goods, and that a full explanation is made, to restore your family's honour.'

Soheila stared at him and began to shake. She said, 'I've seen Zohreh, spoken with her – she still wants revenge – for this is the day, a hundred years ago, when she –'

'Today?' broke in Husam, glancing at Kareen.

'She said Khaled had made a mistake. Today is the anniversary.' She gulped. 'But I didn't want – I didn't

know that – oh, God – I didn't want Khaled to be hurt
– never –'

'Where is he?' snapped Kareen. When Soheila
didn't answer she screamed, 'Where is he, you spawn of
Jehannem?'

'It wasn't me,' said Soheila, quailing before the
Jinn's fury. 'I was attacked in the garden by a man –
Yellow Eyes – Khaled heard, jumped out of the
window, tried to help me – I didn't want – I didn't
know. He took him. He took Khaled.' She began to
shiver uncontrollably, all the accumulated shocks of the
last few days rolling over her in a great wave. 'It's the
truth. The truth, I swear.' Suddenly, everything swam
around her, a roar of black rushed up under her eyelids
and she fell into a dead faint.

Twenty-one

Khaled could hardly breathe. Though his abductor had taken off the gag before bundling him into the boot of the car, there wasn't a great deal of air in there. The ropes cut into his wrists and ankles, and prevented him from moving much. And it was completely dark.

The kidnapper had taken his phone, so he could not call for help. It did not help to yell inside the boot; the solid steel muffled his cries. He had given up on that soon enough, when he discovered it was making him short of breath for no good purpose. Though he had also tried to drum with his feet, especially when he felt the car come to a stop, it had come to nothing. He couldn't be heard over the roar of traffic outside and the gunning of motorbike, car, bus and truck engines at traffic lights.

Now he was beginning to feel more than a little fearful that he might suffocate in the boot before arriving at whatever destination they were headed to. Only prayer was left – and that he had done a lot of.

They had been driving for quite a while. Khaled thought they might be heading north, for once right at the beginning, when they'd stopped at a traffic light, he had heard a voice on a megaphone promoting a big shopping complex in North Jumana. But he wasn't sure if they were still going in that direction, for they had gone through several roundabouts and intersections after that, and were driving steadily along what must be a highway. They must be well out of the city, on the big highway that cut through the desert.

His mind kept going back to one thing: who had kidnapped him, and why? His family had been targeted in the past, but not for a long time. When his father was small someone had abducted him and demanded that Khaled's grandfather pay a large ransom for his safe return. Khaled's grandfather had refused to pay. He had a retinue of loyal nomadic warriors at his command, and he sent them in search of Khaled's father. They soon found the kidnapper – he wasn't a very clever man, a disgruntled former secretary who thought he'd enrich himself the easy way – and rescued Abdullah. As to the kidnapper, Khaled's grandfather had cut him to pieces and scattered him in the desert for the hyenas and vultures to eat. No-one had ever tried to abduct an al-Farouk again, because the story had become widely known – his grandfather had seen to that.

But this was no disgruntled former employee. Khaled had never seen the man before. Yet, strangely, his narrow yellow eyes reminded him of something – of someone, and he couldn't quite work out who.

A sudden thought struck him, making him shake like a leaf. What if this was the curse striking him? What if all their efforts had been in vain?

But it wasn't his birthday today. He mustn't think that way; it would make him panic, and then he'd never be able to escape.

He felt the car turn off the highway and start on a much more bumpy road. He thought, 'We're heading straight into the desert.' Some time passed. He began to feel light-headed; his throat felt tight and sore. At last, the car lurched to a stop. Seconds later, the boot was flung open and a veiled face peered in at him. It wasn't Yellow Eyes but someone else, probably the driver. 'Still alive, eh?' growled the man. He reached in, pulled out Khaled and dumped him unceremoniously on the sand behind the car.

Just as Khaled had thought, they were deep in the desert. Great dunes rose all around them like petrified golden waves. In the distance, under a twisted thorn tree, a black woollen tent, of the kind nomads used, was pitched.

Khaled took great gulps of air. He felt sick to the stomach, and retched several times. The man laughed. 'Not quite the luxury you're used to boy, is it?' He spoke Aksaran, but with a heavy accent: Mesomian, or perhaps Masrikhan.

Khaled found his voice. 'Who are you? I demand you take me back at once.' He tried to sound haughty and commanding but, to his horror, his voice came out like a rusty squeak.

The man laughed. 'Hey, Mahmoud,' he called to his companion, who was coming around the side of the car, 'do you hear his Majesty ordering us to let him go? Still thinks he's in Daddy's palace, eh?'

'Shut up, you fool,' said the other man, the one with the coldly cruel yellow eyes. 'You talk too much.' Ignoring the other's glare, he knelt down beside the boy, and despite his protest, gagged him again. Then he cut the ropes around his ankles, and said, 'Get up. March.' He motioned towards the black tent. Khaled stood up unsteadily.

'Did you hear him? March!' said his friend heartily, and gave Khaled a push. He was a big, beefy man and nearly sent the boy sprawling. The man he'd called Mahmoud glared at Khaled again, but said nothing. Khaled had no option but to do as he was told, for both men were armed with very businesslike-looking guns.

It was hot, and he was panting by the time they reached the tent. They pushed him inside. It was dim and close. There was a worn carpet on the sand, and shabby cushions scattered around. In a corner were several bottles of water and a torch; in another a cardboard box of supermarket food. Khaled's heart leapt. It seemed as if the kidnappers did not want to kill him, or at least not yet. Maybe it wasn't the curse. Perhaps they were after a ransom.

The driver had followed him into the tent. He cut the ropes on Khaled's hands and took the gag off. 'You might be here a while,' he sneered. 'You might as well make yourself comfortable.' He gestured at the water bottles. 'Drink.'

Khaled folded his arms and glared defiantly at his kidnapper. 'I want to know what you want with me.'

'You'll find out soon enough,' said the man, smiling faintly. 'Our boss will be here in a short while to have a little chat with you.'

'Who is your boss?' snapped Khaled. At that moment, Mahmoud pushed his way in. 'Tarik, leave him and go and get the fire going. It's going to be cold out here tonight.'

Beefy Tarik shrugged, but did as he was told. Mahmoud turned on Khaled, a pendant on a chain around his neck catching the light as he swung around. 'And you had better save your breath for later.'

'If you're after money, gangster scum, you're wasting your time, my family never pays ransom,' said Khaled fiercely. 'My father commands the loyalty of a great clan and wherever you hide, you'll be found and put to death.'

Mahmoud punched Khaled in the stomach, making him double up in pain. 'Nobleman of a corrupt and decadent country,' Mahmoud hissed, looming over the boy, 'when our boss arrives, you will give him the answers he wants, or by Jehannem, you will see what I and my friend are most skilled at. We have broken many much stronger, older and braver than you, Ameeratan spawn, with our fire-love.'

'Fire-love?' whispered Khaled.

The man pulled a lighter from his pocket. He clicked it on, very close to Khaled's face. 'The fire will love you,' he said, very softly. 'It will love your hair –' and here he brought it so close to Khaled's hair that he could smell the ends of it crisping and singeing – 'it will love your skin –' and here he skimmed it along Khaled's cheek, making the boy flinch in pain and terror – 'it will love you everywhere. You will die in Lady Fire's sweet embrace, my boy, screaming her name!'

Khaled could not speak or move. His stomach ached where he had been punched; his burnt cheek hurt unbearably; his nostrils were full of the burnt-chicken smell of singed hair. But more than all of that, he was terrified by the look of delighted cruelty in Mahmoud's eyes. No mercy could be expected from this man.

'Please,' Khaled said, unable to keep the tremor from his voice, 'why are you doing this to me? I don't know what you want. I don't know who you are.'

The man put his face very close to Khaled's. His yellow eyes glittered; his breath was curiously hot, sweet and heavy. 'Don't tell lies, boy. You know very well what we're after.' He grabbed Khaled's wrist and gave it a painful twist, making Khaled cry out again. 'And you'd better change your strategy when the boss arrives, or you'll be very sorry.'

'Mahmoud!' Tarik was at the tent flap. 'What are you doing? You know the boss said not to hurt him just yet.'

'Shut up, you fool,' snapped Mahmoud. Nevertheless, he got up and moved away from Khaled.

'Leave the boy. Come and play cards with me,' said Tarik. 'The boss won't be here for hours yet.'

'You and your cards,' said Mahmoud, his yellow eyes still on Khaled, who shrank in on himself.

'He'll keep,' said Tarik, glancing at the terrified boy. 'You'll get your chance, Mahmoud – but right now you'd better stay away from him.'

'I suppose you're right,' said Mahmoud, and gave a horrible little giggle. 'Think about it, nobleman's brat. Think about how much fun we'll have later.'

And with that, he followed Tarik out of the tent, leaving Khaled alone.

For a moment he could not move. 'This is it,' he thought despairingly. 'This is the curse: I am to be tortured to death by wicked, cruel men wielding fire. This is to be my fate – no, no, I must not think that way or I will go mad. I must try and get out of here before their boss arrives. But how? I'm miles out in the desert, and they're just outside the tent, sitting by the fire.'

His thoughts chased themselves round in his head. At home, they'd know he was missing soon enough. Payem would tell them. That is, if Payem hadn't died from that blow on the head. Poor Payem, he must have surprised the kidnapper in the garden. He'd fought bravely, but he was so small and skinny. Tears came to Khaled's eyes and he brushed them away. He looked down at the worn carpet under his feet. If only it were the flying carpet, he thought desperately.

After a while he got up and went to the tent flap and peered out. Dusk had fallen. Mahmoud and Tarik were sitting some distance away by a thorn-tree branch fire, absorbed in their card game. They had turned on their car radio and bouncy pop music was wafting over the otherwise silent desert. All around them, the great dunes rose – the tent itself was pitched right beside one of them. Khaled returned to his cushions to think. The only method of transport out there was the kidnappers' car. He'd had a few driving lessons with Omar and could drive a little. But how could he hope to take the car? Mahmoud and Tarik were posted not far from the tent entrance. They couldn't fail to see him if he tried to run away. Anyway, even if he did manage to get away without them seeing him, what chance was there of survival? If he was right about the direction they had been driving in, this must be the Howling Desert to the north of Jumana, near the border with Mesomia. Hardly any nomads even passed through the Howling Desert. It was real badlands — thirst country with no respite, known to be haunted by evil spirits and carnivorous beasts, and prone to sudden, devastating, howling windstorms that gave the desert its name.

His thoughts jumped to his captors, to Mahmoud especially. His flesh crept. The man's eyes were devoid of humanity — yellow as a predator's, and as blank. And that pendant around his neck — it looked like a wolf's head. Perhaps it was some gang symbol. He frowned. Mahmoud had spoken about a 'corrupt and decadent country'. It didn't sound like the sort of thing someone in a crime gang would say, but more political, more like the rantings of The Vampire, across the border. Perhaps they were agents of The Vampire. But what would Mesomians want with him? His family had never been involved in international politics. Then, with a shock, he remembered what Sharib had said about Mr Harir, the carpet dealer in the bazaar who had disappeared. The old carpet dealer had been killed by Mesomian assassins, and they had been watching the shop . . .

A horrible thought struck him then. What if Sharib himself was a spy for the Mesomians? Surely not. He felt in his bones that the dwarf was to be trusted. He was a good man . . .

With a jolt he suddenly remembered what was familiar about Yellow Eyes's face and voice. They were similar to that of the werewolf Gur Thalab. And

Mahmoud wore that wolf pendant. 'Yellow Eyes is a werewolf, too,' Khaled thought, and stood up in sudden panic. And he must be related to Gur Thalab – the likeness between them was too striking. Perhaps it was Gur Thalab who was Mahmoud's boss. But if that was the case, why hadn't the werewolf attacked him back in the Gold Market? But then Husam and Sharib had been with him . . .

The more he thought about it, the more he became convinced that the men had followed him from the Gold Market. And that could only mean that Gur Thalab had alerted them.

Heart thumping, he looked feverishly around the tent, trying to think of a means of escape.

Twenty-two

The first thing Soheila saw when she recovered consciousness was Farasha hovering above her, his goggle eyes fixed on her face. They looked at each other for an instant, then Farasha squeaked, 'She's awake, she's awake!'

'Are you feeling better, child?' It was Husam's voice. Soheila looked around. She was lying on a soft bed. Around her were Husam, Abdullah and the strange little man. She tried to struggle up, but Husam said, 'You'll feel dizzy if you try to sit up too quickly. Here –' and he arranged a heap of pillows behind Soheila's back.

Memory was returning jerkily to Soheila. She looked at Abdullah, who was pale as death but otherwise composed. Tears sprang into her eyes. She said faintly, 'Oh Shayk, I'm so sorry. Khaled –'

'You must help us, Soheila,' said Abdullah. 'You must tell us if there was anything – anything that distinguished this attacker at all.'

Soheila looked down at her hands. She whispered, 'I remember the man's eyes – yellow eyes, and so cold, so cruel. He was very strong; he had a grip like iron. He was dressed in jeans, a leather jacket, a shirt – and he wore a pendant on a silver chain – a white pendant shaped like an animal's head – I remember now, it was a wolf's head, with red eyes.'

Husam and Kareen looked at each other. Abdullah gave a little gasp. Farasha, whirring about in fright, squeaked, 'A wolf, a wolf! Oh, my young master is in terrible danger, he may be dead. Oh, woe is me! Woe is me!'

'Don't be silly, Farasha,' said Husam, shortly. He turned to Soheila. 'Are you sure it was a wolf's head?'

Soheila nodded. Abdullah gulped, and said, 'The White Wolves – but why? Why? I do not understand why they would ever . . .' He saw their expressions, and explained, almost inaudibly, 'The White Wolves are the most feared hit squad of the Mesomian secret police.'

'The Mesomian secret police!' exclaimed Husam. 'What do they have to do with Zohreh's curse? What could they want with Khaled?'

'I have no idea,' said Abdullah, tiredly, 'but it is said that at least some of the Wolves are not – not natural humans.'

'Werewolves!' said Husam, whirling on Sharib. The little man looked puzzled and very unhappy.

'Now, don't think that –' he began. 'Don't think that Gur Thalab –'

'What is it? What are you saying?' said Abdullah sharply. 'Is it because of your carpet mechanic that my son is in danger?'

'No, no, I can't believe that,' said Sharib. 'Not all werewolves are the same, my lord. Gur Thalab was tortured by those very same White Wolves in the Black Prison. He is no traitor. Perhaps they have taken Khaled because they saw us the other day in the Carpet Bazaar and assumed we were in contact with Harir, and thus enemies of Mesomia.'

'How can that be?' said Abdullah angrily. 'Our family has never been involved in anything to do with Mesomia. We must do something now. Sharib, can't you and your Jinns show us where the White Wolves have taken Khaled?'

'We can try,' said Sharib rather doubtfully. He beckoned to Farasha. 'And I think you can help us.'

'Me?' squealed Farasha, losing height in his agitation and spiralling to the floor. 'Me, Jinn master?'

'Yes, you, Farasha. You have shown an unusual initiative for a Jinn of your caste. I think you can help my tame ones to see a little further.'

'Why don't you ask her?' squeaked Farasha, twitching a whisker at Kareen.

'Because her powers are too great; she would fry up my poor little ones. But you, Farasha, you I think have possibilities. Just think, Farasha, you are one of the great and noble race of Jinn. And you have shown unusual courage and curiosity for one of your usually dull race. Will you not call on every ounce of your powers, every trace of your knowledge, and use it just for these next few minutes? Do you understand?'

Farasha was sitting huddled on the floor, his wings drooping, his whiskers limp. 'I understand,' he said, 'but it has never been done before. What will Brother Bikaj think?'

Kareen snapped, 'Farasha, are you a Jinn, or a miserable insect of no consequence?'

Farasha glared up at her, his pop-eyes fierce. 'How dare you, gypsy creature,' he said haughtily. He flapped up onto Sharib's shoulder. 'I consent,' he said, in the same haughty tone. 'I will do whatever is needful for the house of my lord and his kinsmen.'

'Well spoken,' said Sharib, a smile playing around his lips. 'Now, come into the garden. We must hurry.'

Husam and Abdullah went out at a run, following Sharib and Farasha. Kareen glanced at Soheila, still lying on the bed. 'You had better stay right here,' she said in a harsh tone. 'It's my view they have been very forgiving with you. You told the truth, that I'll grant, but your heart is still riven with bitterness, that I can see. I still don't trust you, Soheila. Do you understand?'

Soheila said nothing. Her stomach churned with sickness; her eyes ached. The Jinn looked at her, harrumphed, and went out, locking the door behind her. Soheila lay quite still for a moment. Then she began to weep hot, burning tears that fell down her thin cheeks like lava. Sobs shook her, years of bitterness about the wrongs done to her family rising in her throat like a terrible wave of black nausea. She sobbed as if her heart would break, as if her very being would crack. In her despair, she felt as if she was going to die, as if she wanted to die. Nothing had any meaning for her any more. She had lived for revenge and now it had been shown to be an ugly and vile and sordid thing. She had sent Khaled to his death at the hands of the hideous Mesomian secret police. She had taken away that kind old man's only child. She had sinned against hospitality and kindness and truth, and what was more, she had failed utterly in her quest for justice. Zohreh would not be appeased, her spirit would not be put to rest, and because of what Soheila had done, the wrong committed against her ancestor would never be compensated. Of that she was sure. The al-Farouks had been more than kind to her, she knew that now. Kareen and Husam's harshness was only what she deserved. And their last remaining shreds of kindness – how it would melt away when they discovered she had lured Khaled into the garden, following Zohreh's instructions. None of them, not even the Jinn, knew about that.

Nothing remained to her – not the thought of the Talisman; not the vision of Zohreh, for now she did not even want to try and call it up. The image of her ancestor did not fill her with admiration and a strong sense of an injustice that must be righted; instead, she felt a sense of creeping horror. Though the silk sachet of Zohreh's ashes still lay against her breast, Soheila had no desire to speak with the old woman again. She could not face those burning, accusing, inhumanly demanding eyes again. And yet she was afraid that now the vengeful spirit would never let her go.

Night falls swift and black in the desert. Soon it was pitch dark outside, with only the fire providing any light. The men still sat by it, playing cards and drinking whisky. They had got up to look at Khaled twice and he seemed to be sleeping so they had left him alone.

But Khaled was not asleep. He was just waiting for them to completely relax. He had decided on a plan. This kind of tent had no floor, only the carpet on the sand. He would burrow out under the tent, out the back, near the dunes. He knew there was little chance of escape in the Howling Desert. He might get lost, or die of thirst. But it was night, and cool. And he knew he could not wait till the Mesomians's boss arrived.

Quietly, he crept to the flap of the tent and looked out. The two men were chatting, laughing, slapping the cards down on the sand. Now was the time . . . He began to burrow out under the tent. The sand was packed quite hard, but he soon managed to dig his way out, emerging at the back of the tent, right up against the dune.

He held his breath and waited for a moment. He could hear the men's voices, chattering companionably, and the sound of the radio. He looked up at the sky, orienting himself by the stars. South was Jumana. That was the direction he must go in.

Suddenly, he thought he heard, far away, the sound of a powerful car engine. Noise travels a long distance in the desert and there was no telling how far away the car was. But Khaled knew he did not have much time left. He must leave straight away.

The desert is a dangerous place. But Khaled's people had lived in hardship in the desert for centuries before they had become wealthy and built great cities. They had never tamed the desert, but they had come to know it intimately.

'We lived in howling wildernesses like this one,' thought Khaled. 'We found God in them. And Father has often taken me into the desert; he always felt the al-Farouks should never lose sight of the fact it had once been our home. I will survive, God willing.'

He climbed the dune, swiftly, silently. At the top he crouched down and looked back. Mahmoud and Tarik were still sitting by the fire. They had noticed nothing. Then he looked south and saw a pair of headlights coming over the desert, still a long way away. An icy hand gripped at his heart. He could not go south. He must go north – they would not expect him to go that way. A slight breeze had arisen, so the shifting sand would wipe out his footprints – but heading north was still a dangerous thing to do, for he had never been further north before and would have no idea where he was going.

Suddenly, the thought came to him of Melkior, Zohreh's ancestor, who had travelled so far to find the baby king of his prophecy, the prophecy of the stars. He remembered the warmth of the Talisman in his hand. It had been a thing of beauty and wonder, not a thing of revenge. There would be no point in trying to reach the spirit of Zohreh, for she was an unquiet, vengeful spirit, restlessly seeking the pain of others who had personally done nothing to her. But her great ancestor, the legendary Magvanda, he had been granted a great treasure, a thing born in love and peace. Perhaps, just perhaps . . .

'I will restore it,' he whispered to the silent stars. 'I promise you, Melkior, I will make it my life's work to find your family, restore your treasure to them, and repay them for the evil that was done. I promise, Melkior of the Stars, that honour and peace and comfort shall be theirs again.'

It seemed to him that one star began to shine more brightly than the others. He thought he saw it spin, once, then remain still again, its light shining very brightly, hanging over the northern horizon like a guiding light.

Twenty-three

Soheila was lying face down on the bed, all her tears spent, when she heard a loud scrabbling noise, and someone sprang lithely into the room through the open window.

He was one of the most striking-looking people Soheila had ever seen: a tall, powerful young man with amber eyes of unusual brilliance, an aquiline nose, and thick chestnut hair with one single lock of white in it, that framed a high–cheekboned, creamy-coloured face under a green turban. His teeth were very white and rather pointed. He was dressed in baggy green trousers, an embroidered green jacket fastened at the waist with a cummerbund, and a swirling black cloak. He had a thick chestnut moustache that drooped at the ends, and a single, large gold ring glittered on his powerful-looking hands. On the ring was a symbol Soheila recognised.

'Who – who are you?' she stammered, staring at him.

He bowed. 'I am Gur Thalab al Kutroob, of the

Kirtis Mountains,' he said in a low, beautiful voice. 'Don't be afraid. I was standing outside the window and heard everything. I have come to help you.'

'To help me?' said Soheila, finding her voice at last. 'What do you mean?'

'To help you repair what you have done.'

'I – I don't understand. Who are you?'

'I've told you,' said Gur, smiling faintly.

'But –' She looked at the ring, and the wolf's head imprinted on it.

'I am a werewolf,' said Gur. 'It is my curse, and my burden. I know what it is to be born to endless night, to be hostage to others' sins. I know you are suffering, and want with all your heart to repair the damage you have caused. And so I have come to help you.'

Soheila looked up into his golden eyes. 'But the White Wolves have taken Khaled.'

'I heard that, too.' The young man's eyes glittered. 'Even more reason for me to want to help you. I have accounts to settle with them, for though they are members of my own clan, they have betrayed me and many of my kin.'

Soheila was about to speak when the door burst open and Husam came rushing in. 'I heard a noise,' he began, then stopped when he saw Gur Thalab. His eyes narrowed. 'Who are you?'

'Gur Thalab al Kutroob,' said the werewolf lord. 'You met me in the Gold Market, friend.'

'Gur Thalab,' said Husam, 'but I thought —'

'I was deep in melancholia then,' said the werewolf. 'The change had come on me and I did not want anyone to see me in the guise of a foul beast. But the carpet you and Khaled brought to my workshop has accomplished a miracle for me.' He pointed out the window to the garden and said, 'It is just outside. Come, I will show you.'

Farasha shot up out of Husam's pocket, where he had been hiding. 'No, no, no! Don't do as he says. It's a trick.'

'No trick, I promise, little Jinn,' said Gur Thalab, smiling and showing his beautiful white teeth. 'You come too, and protect them, if you're worried.'

Farasha puffed himself up. 'That I will.'

'We will all feel much safer then,' said Husam, winking at Soheila. She gave a tiny smile, as if hardly daring to.

There lay the carpet, unrolled on the path and Husam could not help staring. It was completely different. Not only was it clean but the birds on it looked much finer, much more subtle, their colours rich and glowing, not garish and gaudy any more. Gur Thalab smiled at his astonishment.

'I have my own very potent mixtures of magical herbs — a mixture of marshland and mountain plants — to clean flying carpets, and as I worked on it, I discovered that the design that was apparent to the naked eye

actually overlaid another.' He knelt down to the carpet
and gently touched the beautiful red-gold plumage of
the woven birds. Whether it was her imagination or
not, Soheila thought that the birds moved a little under
the werewolf prince's touch. 'These are true firebirds,'
he said. 'Their real shape was hidden under the other
clumsy design, to hide their real purpose from the eyes
of traitors and spies and informers.' He looked up at
them with shining eyes. 'This carpet was made by a
very great Enchantress. Though she was young, its
spirit is very old. It not only helps whoever flies on it
to go wherever it is he needs to go; it also infuses
whoever touches it with courage and strength.'

'But,' said Husam uncertainly, 'it – er – well, it
failed us, dumped us in Shideh instead of taking us all
the way to Jumana. We had to take a ship instead, over
the gulf.'

'Could it be that the carpet took you where you
needed to go, not precisely where you *wanted* to go?
Perhaps you were needed in Shideh for some reason,
and so the carpet homed in there.'

'I doubt it!' snorted Husam and was about to go on
when the expression in Soheila's eyes stopped him.
Very softly, her eyes on the carpet, the girl said,
'Whatever it was, I am glad. For otherwise I would not
have met you.'

'I do not know if it was intended. But no matter,'
said Gur Thalab. 'Flying carpets are like silent Jinn,' he

went on, looking sideways at an intent Farasha, who was minutely examining the carpet design. 'They are programmed to fulfil a particular task, carefully calibrated to fly where you want to go. But this one –' he stroked one of the birds again, and this time Soheila distinctly saw plumage ripple under his hand – 'has yet another feature. The Carpet Enchantress wove a special formula into it, which I recognised at once, for it is the motto of my house: *Touch if you dare*. It is a motto that has been banned from sight in Mesomia since The Vampire took over, killed my father the Arga and installed my usurping uncle in his place. The carpet was calling to me, my friends! And I knew at once that the long wait was over; that my country needed me; that I must travel to the Marshlands and find the Enchantress who had made the carpet. This discovery is what broke through my melancholia and made the wolf-madness leave me so soon.' He looked at them, eyebrows raised, a smile on his handsome face. 'I must confess, I wanted the carpet to fly me to the Marshlands straight away, but it took me here, where I obviously needed to be.'

'Well, well,' said Husam, 'if that thief in Kapalau had realised what a beauty it was, he'd never have let it go for what we paid for it!'

Just then, Kareen, Sharib and Abdullah came rushing into the garden. They stopped abruptly, and stared at the carpet and Gur Thalab. Husam thought that it was the first time he had ever seen Kareen disconcerted.

'What a fool! How could I have been so blind?' Kareen said without preamble, shaking her head. She looked at Gur Thalab. 'You are the one who did this?'

'I am,' he said.

'You are the carpet mechanic? Yet by your accent and dress, you are a prince of the Kirtis Mountains,' Abdullah said, bewildered, coming towards Gur Thalab.

'Of course he is,' said Kareen impatiently, squatting down to look closely at the carpet, 'he is both, that's all. And he is of the legendary werewolf clan. I have heard much of your people,' she went on. 'I am glad you are on our side.'

'Not all of us are,' acknowledged Gur Thalab. 'There is no time to lose now. We should take the flying carpet and go and find Khaled. I will come with you.' He bared his teeth. 'I will be glad to have the chance to fight the White Wolves once more. I have hidden myself away for too long.'

Husam said, 'Have you found the precise directions yet, Sharib?'

Sharib sighed. 'I've had difficulties because the White Wolf who abducted Khaled didn't leave behind any objects that he touched. Farasha's tried hard to focus extra power on the Jinns but so far we've come up with nothing.'

'What about me?' said Soheila suddenly. 'He touched me, remember.'

Everyone stared at her. Sharib hit his forehead and gave a loud cry. 'What a fool I've been!' he said. 'Of course, you're quite right. Let's go to the very spot where he attacked you, Soheila, and we'll direct the Jinns from you. Oh, and take the carpet too. You might need to take off very quickly.'

Sharib wound the watch back to the approximate time Soheila had been attacked and asked the Jinn of the Watch to show them what had happened at that time. He stood with Farasha on his shoulder and a hand on one of Soheila's shoulder, holding the Jinn of the Watch in his other hand. Everyone crowded around. Just visible in one corner of the watch face was the garden wall, and a black-clad figure slipping down it.

'Quick, Soheila, the Jinn of the Phone, get it out of my top pocket, we want to hear what's going on.'

Soheila did as she was told. 'Hit the button,' said Sharib, and as soon as she did, the Jinn of the Phone said, 'I am the Jinn of the Phone, and your faithful servant. What do you want to hear?'

'Everything that moves in the watch face,' said Sharib, and all at once, spookily, they could hear sounds – a foot scraping the wall, a breath, the swish of a rope ladder. The figure in the watch face turned. They saw a black-veiled face and yellow, gleaming, cruel eyes.

Gur Thalab stiffened and a low growl began in his throat. Sharib pushed the mobile closer to the watch so that it hung almost directly over the spot where the man was sliding down into the garden. A stone shifted against his feet, a twig cracked. The mobile crackled and they suddenly heard, clear and cold, a voice, cursing in accented Aksaran.

'That is a man from my land,' said Gur. 'It is a man from my own werewolf clan.'

'The glasses,' panted Sharib, 'Husam, they're on my arm, quick, unhook them, put them on my nose.'

Husam did so and Sharib, the glasses on his nose, bent over the watch and said, 'Jinn of the Glasses, do not lose that man from sight, whatever you do.'

'I hear and obey,' came the voice of the Jinn, and the lenses clouded over at once, then went reflective, mirroring the action in the watch face.

Soheila came into the garden and was set upon, and Khaled tried to rescue her, the sound of his struggle clearly heard over the phone. Combining the power of all the Jinns, as if he were an earth to electrical current, Sharib was sweating and panting, his face losing all colour, his limbs beginning to shake; this was clearly not an easy task for him. On his shoulder, Farasha shook and shivered, all his tiny being concentrated on pushing his fellow Jinns further and further, deepening their power. The thug was just over the wall with his burden when suddenly Sharib gave a hoarse cry and fell, the watch flying out of his hands, the glasses off his nose. Farasha flapped weakly off his shoulder. The phone, which Soheila was still holding, gave a great crackling spurt, a roar, then flew out of her hand and came to rest by Sharib, sputtering and blinking to itself.

'Sharib!' They all knelt by him. The Jinn master was out cold.

'We'll lose them!' shouted Abdullah, beside himself.

Gur Thalab bent down and picked up the glasses, pushed them onto his nose, and shouted imperiously, 'Keep that man in sight, as your master said.'

Amazingly, Farasha lifted up his head and said, 'Wait, I will help you, wolf prince.' Painfully, he crept up to Gur Thalab's arm. 'Oh Jinn of the Glasses,' he croaked, 'this is the most important task you've ever done. Concentrate, concentrate! Harder! I will help you!'

'I hear and obey,' said the Jinn meekly.

In the twin mirrors of the glasses they could see the driver of the car, Khaled being thrown into the boot, and his abductor jumping into the front seat and slamming the door. The car took off at great speed, racing through the streets of Jumana towards the north. They saw it leave the city limits, saw it tearing up the highway, then turn off onto the sidetrack. They saw a black tent loom up. Khaled was bundled out and marched to the tent. All at once, the lenses went blank again, and though Gur shook them, the picture obstinately refused to come back. Abdullah, who had been watching impatiently, said, 'Enough! We know he was taken to the Howling Desert – I know the direction they went. We must go at once and rescue him.'

'We must use the carpet,' said Husam. 'Gur, Kareen, come with me. We will fight the Wolves and rescue Khaled.'

'My days as a fighter are over, and I would only be in the way,' said Abdullah, his colour high, 'as much as I would like to strangle those wretches with my bare hands. I will inform the Prince of what has happened, and pray for your safe return.'

Soheila blurted out, 'Please, let me come with you to find Khaled. Please.'

'You, come with us?' snapped Kareen.

'This will be too dangerous –' began Husam, but Gur stopped him.

'She must come,' he said quietly. 'It is only right.'

Kareen shot Soheila a suspicious glance, but said nothing, merely shrugged. 'We must be back by midnight,' she said. Quickly, she told Soheila about the advice Ebon Zarah had given her.

Soheila whispered, 'If we are back by midnight Khaled and I will call up my ancestor, together, and beg her to end the curse.'

They all looked at her. Abdullah said, 'Go with my blessing then, my child; help to bring my son back safely.' He paused. 'I think you will need the treasure of your house, to tackle such a task. You need to take the Talisman with you. Farasha, please take Kareen and tell Bikaj I ask he give the Talisman to her.'

'I'll do that,' said Farasha, excitedly, and flapped swiftly off, followed by Kareen. Soheila gulped and looked at Abdullah. 'My lord,' she said, 'there is something I must tell you –'

'Tell me when you bring my son back, child,' said Abdullah, a tired smile lightening his face. 'Tell me then. I do not need to know, now.' He paused and turned to Husam and Gur. 'Bring him back safely, my friends; he is the light of my heart.'

'Don't worry,' said Husam, clasping Abdullah's hands. 'He will be back here, safe, before you know it.'

'I hope so. I pray to God it may be so,' said Abdullah, and just then, Farasha and Kareen came back. Kareen had the Talisman in her hands. Without speaking, she handed it to Soheila.

As Soheila took the box in trembling hands and gently opened it, an extraordinary radiance seemed to emerge from the box, lighting up Soheila's face, smoothing out its harsh lines, its unchildlike gauntness. In that radiance, it seemed to them they could see the face of a man, a man in a great white turban, with startlingly blue eyes under waves of iron-grey hair.

Soheila said, 'Oh Melkior – Melkior of the Stars –' and tears rolled down her cheeks. A voice said, 'It is well, daughter, it is well. I will guide you.' As the echoes of the voice died away, the radiance began to fade. But

Soheila stood there with the box in her hand, the tears still rolling down her cheeks.

At last, she turned to Abdullah and said, 'One hundred years ago, on this very day, Zohreh was slain in this house. Tonight, Khaled and I will stand together, our hands on the treasure of my house, and we will lay my ancestor's spirit to rest. She is a vengeful spirit, still, but I will lay her to rest, that I promise you, and bring this curse to an end, forever.'

'I hope to God you will not be too late,' said Abdullah, much moved. 'Please bring me back my dear one.' And with that, he turned away, so that none of them should see the tears in his eyes.

'I will come with you, my lord,' said Farasha, flapping up onto the old man's shoulder. 'I will help to protect this house, and keep you company, till they all return.'

'I am grateful, Farasha,' said Abdullah very gently. 'You are a true-hearted Jinn, the best of this house.'

Then he turned on his heel and walked away, his back straight, his head high, Farasha riding proudly on his shoulder. There was a short silence.

'As to me, I'd better try and rescue my Jinns before the night's out, or I won't be able to call myself a Jinn master any longer,' said Sharib, who had groggily come to his senses. He watched as Gur, Husam, Kareen and Soheila, clutching the Talisman, climbed onto the carpet. At a whispered word from the werewolf lord, it rose up into the air and straight over the garden wall, into the night. Sharib watched till they were out of sight, then, sighing, bent down to gather up the scattered pieces of his Jinn housing. It would be a long night.

Twenty-four

Khaled had been walking for about an hour in the desert when he began to hear a peculiar sound. He stopped and listened. It was not, as he had at first feared, the engine of a pursuing car. It was something else — a dull roar. What could it be?

He looked up at the sky. The bright star he thought of as Melkior's still shone brightly in the north, guiding him. The desert was silent around him. So far, he had met none of its feared denizens — not desert lions, not hyenas, not, most feared of all, afreets, evil Jinn who were said to roam this place.

It's not easy walking in sand dunes, even when, like Khaled, you are not a stranger to the desert. There were moments when he stumbled and almost fell. Sheer walls of glittering sand rose up in front of him like unstable, endless mountains, and he had to scramble up them, his calf muscles aching with the strain. He took a sip of water from time to time, trying to conserve as much as he could for the daytime. He had no idea how long it would take to walk out of here. He presumed they wouldn't have taken him too deep into the desert – they hadn't had time – but it is always slower walking in sand. And even if he managed to elude pursuit tonight, would he have managed to get somewhere more hospitable by daybreak, when the sun would rise and gradually fill the desert with its pitiless light?

He slogged up another dune. It seemed to him the sound was getting louder. He frowned. The roar was changing tone. There was a kind of wild shriek to it, a sort of –

He froze. Just below him, in the starlight, he could see something moving. A long, fluid silver form, full of feline grace. 'Desert lion!' thought Khaled. It was pointless trying to think of defending himself against it. He had no weapon. His only chance was to stay very quiet and still. If he made a move, the creature would see him and attack.

The lion seemed nervous. Its tail switched. Its broad face was turned up to the sky, as if examining it. Its soft, heavy big-cat paws scratched at the sand. Then Khaled heard it growl, deep in its throat. In the next instant, it was bounding up the slope, towards Khaled. The boy's heart nearly threw itself out of his chest, but he forced himself to stay still. The desert lion reached him. Its narrow, green eyes looked straight into his: for an instant, both boy and animal seemed suspended in time. Then the creature gave a deep, throaty roar, leapt past Khaled in a single bound, and disappeared up the crest of the dune and down the other side.

Khaled had no time to wonder what had happened to spook the lion. In the next instant, a howling and a shrieking and a roar were upon him, as of twenty thousand demons all speaking at once, and he found himself picked up as if by an invisible hand, into the whirling, hot heart of a terrible wind.

It was Kareen who first spotted the tent – and the headlights of the car, racing along the desert track towards it. 'It's them!' she shouted, over the gathering noise of the wind. She peered down. 'I can see the tent, and people by a fire. Follow me.' Rapidly transforming into a great red bird, she swooped down from the carpet into the black night. Gur Thalab, who was steering the carpet, yelled, 'Hold on tightly, I'm going straight down!' In the next instant, the carpet plunged sickeningly, flying fast as lightning after Kareen.

The two men by the fire only had time to glance up and let out a startled exclamation when the Jinn was on them, bird claws pointed straight at their eyes. Then the carpet flopped down on the sand, disgorging its passengers rather abruptly. Things happened very quickly then. Gur Thalab was up at once, and in his hand there was a dagger, shining bright and wicked in the moonlight. With a yell that was half a howl, he flung himself at Mahmoud, screaming curses in his own language. But the man was quick; in an instant, he had ducked and feinted, and pulled a small gun from his pocket. He fired, once, and Gur Thalab fell, red blossoming in his side. Husam scrambled up, the old executioner whirling his sword above his head. Shrieking, 'Stay on the carpet, don't put the Talisman at risk!' at Soheila, he sliced at Mahmoud before the man could fire again. His weapon tore at the thug's shoulder, making his gun fly out of his hand. The other thug, Tarik, forehead streaming with blood from the Jinn's attack, staggered around blindly.

The car stopped and two men jumped out – a very large man dressed in white robes, his headcloth pulled up around his face, and a fat, dapper man in a dark suit and dark glasses. Each of them had a gun and they began firing as soon as they got out of the car. Kareen yelled, 'Everyone, get back on the carpet, push the protective shield up, it will stop the bullets. I'll deal with them.' Husam took no notice, and Kareen, seeing this, stood in front of him, spreading her flaming wings so wide that the light from them dazzled the gunmen, who fell back. Then she swooped on the white-robed man, flying straight at his face. Instinctively, he threw his hands up, and dropped his gun. Kareen touched it with the tip of her wing and instantly it burst into flames and exploded, setting the man's robes on fire. Shrieking, he ran away and rolled in the sand, but was engulfed in an instant. Seeing this, the dapper man ran round the back of the car, Husam hot on his heels, his sword held high. Meanwhile, Soheila, disregarding Husam's advice not to move, dragged Gur Thalab's unconscious body to the safety of the carpet. After a struggle, she finally got him on, and laid the Talisman by his side, near the bloody wound.

The dapper man fired. But his shot went wide and Husam knocked him down with the flat of his sword. He sprang at the man, whose gun went flying. But just as Husam grabbed him, the man jerked up, a wicked little dagger in his hand. Husam parried just in time, and now the man gave a great gulping sigh, and fell from a sword-thrust to the heart.

Soheila gave a warning cry: Tarik was sneaking up on Husam, dagger in hand. With a roar of flame, Kareen tackled him, and he fell, screaming, then lay still. Mahmoud, who had groggily recovered, flung his arms up. 'I surrender! I surrender!' he yelled. His yellow eyes were frightened now.

'Just as well for you,' said Husam grimly. He trussed the man up thoroughly with rope he took from the thugs' car. Meanwhile, Soheila had run to the tent. She hadn't really expected to find Khaled there – surely he would have called out to them. But until she looked in and saw nobody was there, she hadn't realised how afraid she'd been of getting there and finding it was no live boy but a dead body that lay there in the tent.

'No-one's here,' she told Kareen, who, having returned to her normal shape, stood behind her, looking in. Kareen nodded. 'That thing will have to tell us,' she said, gesturing towards Mahmoud.

'He got away,' said the cowering prisoner. 'I don't know how. I didn't see him go. It's only desert around here. And he's on foot.'

Soheila had been examing the back of the tent. 'A hole's been dug here,' she said. 'He must have burrowed out.' She looked at the dune behind the tent. 'He must have climbed that.'

Husam bit at his lip. 'Yes. But what direction could he have gone in after that?'

'Let's get on the carpet,' said Kareen. 'We can fly over the whole area, see if we can see him. We can cover a lot of ground quickly in it, much quicker than one boy can walk. I think he would have gone south, towards Jumana.'

'Makes sense. Let's go. But first let's secure that one.' Husam pointed to Mahmoud. He trussed the man up even more securely and locked him in one of the cars. 'He'll keep till we return,' said Husam.

They took off rather jerkily into the gathering wind-storm, until Kareen caught a slipstream of air and settled into a steady cruise, so steady that Gur Thalab remained unconscious. The trouble was that though the carpet flew straight and true, and they were protected from the worst effects of the wind by the bubble of protection, the dizzying whirl of sand thrown up by the wind made it very hard to see down below, even though Kareen had turned on all the lights.

Husam was grim-faced. 'If Khaled is caught in this storm we might never find him – alive or dead.'

'I think we're going the wrong way,' said Soheila. 'I think Khaled would have more likely gone north. You see, the Mesomians were based in Jumana, and that car came from the south. He wouldn't be wanting to walk straight into their path.'

'But north is towards Mesomia –' said Husam.

'Yes, and so they wouldn't think of him going that way.'

Kareen nodded. 'The girl is right,' she said, and turned the carpet around so fast that they were all tumbled into the middle.

For a while, Khaled had existed only in a whirl of noise, a roll of hot dust. He had been tumbled over and over in the grip of the wind, shaken in its howling waves like a bit of driftwood tossed in the ocean. He'd managed at one point to pull down his head-cloth so that it covered his nose and mouth, but though he'd tried to press his feet into the sand to gain a foothold, he'd been whipped off his feet more than once. Khaled knew these winds didn't last more than half an hour or so, but that they could do immense damage. They had been known to swallow up entire encampments of nomads, to sweep great camel caravans off their feet, and to change the whole shape of the desert.

He needed shelter – protection from the pull and snatch of the wind. The dunes were no use. There were no trees anywhere. Only his headcloth and his robe stood between him and the demonic power of the hot wind. And they wouldn't last long. Worst of all, his water bottle was filling up with sand. In just a few hours it would be day and the sun would take possession of the desert again. If the wind hadn't crushed him, the sun would, for sure. Its fiery passage through the sky would mark his end, he thought. Tomorrow was his fifteenth birthday. Zohreh's curse would be accomplished. As she had foretold, he would die by fire – under the burning endless fire of the desert sun, maddened by thirst and weariness.

The sky was completely obscured by the whirling sand. He could no longer see the star or its guiding light. He was completely disoriented, and no longer knew where north was. Even when the fury of the wind abated a little and he could walk, he had no idea if he was walking in the right direction, or if he was going around in circles. Real terror began to fill him, terror of the knowledge of what awaited him. What a fool he'd been to think he could work against fate. What a fool he'd been to think one could make bargains with vengeful spirits. It was obvious Zohreh's spirit was not going to let him go, that he was destined to die and could not escape.

In his present peril, he had almost forgotten about the kidnappers. Then, as the howling of the wind started to die down, it seemed to him that he could hear another sound: a humming, coming closer and closer. Panic filled him. Was it the kidnappers' car? Or did they have some other thing – a helicopter perhaps – out looking for him?

The wind was still blowing but nowhere near as hard as before. He had thought he'd feel relief when at last it stopped, but now he was willing it to go on. At least they wouldn't be able to see him. Where could he hide? He looked up into the sky – and saw a set of powerful lights rushing down at him. They were almost on him. With an anguished yelp, he flung himself flat on the ground and, covering his face with his head cloth, began frantically to dig himself a hiding place in a windswept drift of dune.

Soheila held the Talisman in the palm of her open hand. A soft glow radiated from it into the night. Her eyes wide open, she murmured soft prayers to Akamenia, and asked for the intercession of Melkior and the protection of the Talisman, not just for herself, but for the others on the flying carpet, and Khaled, lost in the howling wastes of wind and sand. She spoke Khaled's name again and again, knowing as she did that something now spoke in her heart for him, that somehow he had changed her life forever.

All at once, she gave a cry. 'Husam! Kareen! I can see something white. Down there, look. It's Khaled. He's fighting the wind, but he's getting tired. Hurry, hurry!'

The hum grew louder and louder, closer and closer, the lights more blinding. Khaled waited, throat dry, heart thumping, in the suffocating silence of his sandy hidey-hole. He waited for the helicopter to set down and for armed thugs to get out and search for him. Instead, he heard the hum stop, and then a voice he hadn't expected at all.

'Are you sure it's him? Hard to see in this place . . .'

'Husam!' Khaled yelled, jumping out of the hole like a jack-in-the-box, scattering sand in every direction, and making both Husam and Soheila shout in sudden fright, though Kareen merely frowned. 'It's me! It's me!' he shouted. 'Oh, you've got the carpet. It works now.' He stared at Soheila, then at Gur Thalab, still lying senseless on the carpet.

Husam said, 'He is our friend, who lies wounded for having helped us.'

Khaled nodded rather absently, his eyes returning to Soheila. 'Payem?' he said, questioningly, his bewildered eyes taking in Soheila's strangely altered appearance, and the box in her hand.

'Not Payem. Meet Soheila,' said Husam, as Soheila, staring at Khaled, went first red, then very white.

'Soheila?'

'I am Soheila of the Melkior clan, Zohreh's great-great-great-grand-daughter, as you are Kassim's great-great-great-grandson,' said Soheila in a very small voice.

'Oh.' It was Khaled's turn to flush, then grow pale. He could not tear his eyes away from her startling blue gaze. His heart gave a little leap, and he didn't know why.

'Forgive me,' said Soheila, 'for not telling you the truth from the start. But I couldn't. You see –'

'She wanted to avenge her ancestor,' said Husam. 'Didn't know about the curse.'

'Oh,' said Khaled again. 'Then you – then you wanted – to – to –'

'I am sorry,' said Soheila, her voice low. 'It was very wrong and I ask your forgiveness, Khaled.'

'Oh no, there is nothing to forgive,' said Khaled. 'It was my family who owed a debt to yours, that should have been repaid long ago. Soheila,' he thought, stupidly. 'Soheila, that is her name, this girl with the huge, deep blue eyes.'

'She had nothing to do with the kidnapping,' said Husam. 'She was just a poor soul, adrift in the world, as so many are. But she found you, as you found her.'

'Yes,' whispered Khaled, and his eyes met Soheila's. She was the first to look away, her heart thumping with an emotion she didn't yet recognise.

At their feet, Gur Thalab stirred. He put a hand to his side, where the wound seemed to have stopped bleeding. His eyes flew open. Khaled said, wonderingly, 'Oh, it is you, Prince Gur. It is you!'

'You recognise me,' whispered Gur hoarsely.

'Of course I do,' said Khaled. 'Who could ever forget you?'

'But the guise you met me in, in the Gold Market.'

'Your eyes are the same, sir,' said Khaled, 'none could mistake them. I am sorry,' he went on, after a short while, 'but for a while I thought you were in league with those others –'

Gur's eyes flashed, then he smiled, wearily and rather sweetly. 'I understand. Why should you not think so, when one of them was of my clan?'

'Mahmoud?' said Khaled.

Gur Thalab nodded. 'He is a cousin, I am afraid.'

'Come on,' said Kareen impatiently. 'We've got to get that renegade cousin of yours, Gur, and get back to Jumana as soon as possible. The Prince will be anxious to question him.'

'And your father is waiting anxiously for your

return,' smiled Husam as Khaled settled himself on the carpet.

'As am I,' said Khaled, his eyes on Soheila, who hardly dared look at him.

They were back at the kidnappers' camp in a short while. Even as they approached they could see that something dramatic had happened. Fire had engulfed the cars and the tent, which were burning fiercely. There was no sign of life at all. They circled the area, but the fire was too fierce to be approached.

'He had a lighter,' Khaled said. 'Simple enough to open the petrol cap and set fire to it all.'

'But he was trussed up,' said Husam, staring down at the inferno below. Gur Thalab said, 'Where did you leave him?'

'In the back seat,' said Husam, frowning.

'He must have called on the change to come on him,' said Gur Thalab. 'That moment of change, the instant when you turn from man to wolf, gives you superhuman strength and speed. He would have used that to burst his bonds, smash the glass, get out and light the fires, in those few seconds before he became a wolf. And now he's probably streaking away through the desert, on his way back to Mesomia. We should go after him.'

'No,' said Husam. 'We must go back to Jumana. Khaled is exhausted, Abdullah worried sick. The Prince will be informed of all that has happened. He can send investigators out here to sift through the wreckage. Mahmoud will die in the desert, man or wolf.'

'Perhaps,' said Gur Thalab, rather faintly. 'And perhaps he will not. Anyway, there will always be more Mahmouds, in The Vampire's Mesomia. When I am recovered, I will go back myself, to deal with the evil at its source. I will no longer allow them to turn me into a hunted fugitive, but take on the mantle I should never have abandoned as prince of my people and defender of their freedom.'

He looked at the others. 'And for putting the heart back in me to do that, I have you to thank. I will never forget it.'

Twenty-five

On the way back to Jumana, Soheila thought of the future. She would do her utmost to see that the curse was finally lifted. She would return to Parsari, to her parents who must be sick with worry about her disappearance. She would take up her studies in music again. She would no longer brood about past injustices, but try to bring honour and respect back to the name of Melkior. And to do so, she must look forwards, and not back. Oh, not dishonour the past, for the past is where we come from and has helped to make us what we are. But she would take from the past the lessons she needed, and she would forever hold the memory of the kindness and friendship she had been shown here, in this beautiful place which she had thought was the lair of her enemies. She hoped not that her family and the al-Farouks might be true friends, for surely that was too much to ask, but that they would think of each other with respect and understanding, and without any bitterness at all. She could not ask for any more, though her heart ached at the thought of leaving Khaled. He had become important to her – someone to know better, even a true friend, such as she had never had.

Khaled, for his part, could hardly think at all. He was so aware on the way back of the presence of Soheila, and of the Talisman, that nothing else seemed quite real, and certainly not the fact that in a few hours he'd be fifteen. He tried to concentrate on what he'd say to his father when he got back, and what they could possibly do to repair the wrong that had been done to Soheila's family. But it was hard to think straight. He was so tired. And his heart was full of confusion. He did not know if he was happy or sad or merely anxious or numb.

When they landed at the palace Abdullah came running out to meet them. Forgetting his dignity in his joy, Khaled threw himself into his father's arms. For a moment, father and son were speechless, hugging, kissing, weeping a little.

Then Abdullah spoke. 'There will of course be reparations, Soheila,' he said, an arm around his son, holding him tight as if he would never let him go. 'Now we know you, and we know where to find your kin. We will pay for all the goods Kassim stole, with a hundred years' worth of interest; it should be enough to set you and your family up in great comfort for the rest of your lives. And we will make public the true story of what Kassim did, and how he besmirched your ancestor's honour by telling lies about her.' He paused. 'We hope that you might find it in your heart to help us permanently efface the curse by going with my son to see the Recorder of the Emerald Mountain of Kaf.'

Soheila had not spoken, just looked at them all with those bright blue eyes that concealed as much as they revealed.

Khaled felt his heart constrict as he said, 'We are in your hands, Soheila. It must be your choice. Even should you choose not to forgive us, nor go with me to the Recorder, we will do all in our power to discharge our debts, isn't that so, Father?'

'Indeed,' said Abdullah solemnly.

There was a silence. Everyone stared at Soheila. Finally she said, 'I think we are wasting time standing here. It is close to midnight, and Kareen has said the flower will soon fade.' She looked at Khaled full in the face. 'Will you come with me to the library and stand before the mirror with me while I call the spirit of my ancestor? For it is she who must give us permission to go to the Emerald Mountain. Without her, we will never make it there.'

'We will go with you,' said Abdullah, and Husam agreed.

Soheila shook her head. 'No, it must be just Khaled and I,' she said quietly, but with such determination in her voice that they knew it was pointless to argue. She looked at Khaled, and her voice was a little more uncertain then as she said, 'Will you come with me? I – I do not think there is anything to be afraid of, for we will put our hands together, on the Talisman of the Star, and the spirit of my ancestor Melkior will stand guard over us. Zohreh is a vengeful spirit, but she also wants rest. I am sure of it. Khaled?'

'Of course I'll come,' he said, in a choked voice. 'I – I'm just – sorry, I cannot speak.' He looked into Soheila's face, and those watching saw the same smile dawn deep down in both the young people's eyes.

They stood together in front of the tall carved mirror in the library while behind the closed door, Abdullah and Husam and the others waited anxiously. Soheila was wearing Ebon Zarah's skyflower in her hair. They held the Talisman between them, the box still closed. It was very quiet. The silver light of the moon poured in through the fretted windows, striping the floor with shadow and light. They looked at the clock on the wall. Five minutes to go; four minutes to go; three minutes to go.

'How cold it is,' thought Khaled, shivering without even knowing he was doing it. 'How cold, except for Soheila's fingers on mine.' Two minutes to go; one minute to go.

'How terrified I am,' thought Soheila. 'Utter terror

fills me, much greater than I have ever known. Terror – and yet it is my revered ancestor I'm going to call, the one in whose name I have lived for so much of my life. All that keeps me steady is the touch of Khaled's fingers on mine, as we hold the Talisman.'

The clock began to strike twelve. At the same moment, Soheila whispered, 'Let me speak, Khaled. Say nothing at first. We'll open the Talisman – now!'

The Talisman lay open between them, and a soft light seemed to gently radiate from it. Soheila looked into the mirror and said, 'Oh Zohreh of the Melkior clan, Grandmother of Grandmothers, I beg you to answer my call. It is midnight and I wear a skyflower in my hair. It was midnight a hundred years to the day in which you departed this life. Grandmother Zohreh, answer my call!'

Soheila and Khaled were reflected in the mirror, but Soheila's reflection was, it seemed, subtly changing. Her face was sharpening, hardening. Her eyes were just as burningly blue, but had an older expression in them. Khaled could hardly form the thought that was agitating within him: Zohreh's face was superimposing itself on Soheila's reflection somehow. Gripped by terror, he cast a quick look sideways at the girl. She hadn't changed. It was only the image in the mirror.

'Grandmother of Grandmothers,' said Soheila softly, 'please hear me. We must end the curse forever, oh my beloved ancestor, for the descendants of the man who did you much wrong are nothing like him. They will pay full compensation to the Melkior clan and ensure that your memory is restored to honour here as in your own land.'

Then Soheila fell silent. Khaled turned to look at her and could see tears starting at the corners of her eyes. He turned back to the mirror. He could see the reflection more clearly by the second: Soheila's real form now a shadow behind that of the old woman's. The old woman had unblinkingly fierce, determined eyes. Her thin lips were moving but he could not hear what she was saying. She was not looking at him, but straight at Soheila.

The girl was cold all over with the onslaught of the old woman's disappointed fury. She was accusing Soheila of treachery, of forgetting her, of being a coward. Soheila stayed quiet, though each barb stung her deeply. Soheila reminded herself that Zohreh could not act against the good power of the Talisman and the protection of the skyflower. She could feel the pressure of Khaled's fingers still on hers, and it gave her courage to withstand Zohreh's rage.

Suddenly she gasped, and so did Khaled, for the mirror glass seemed to thicken, to mist over; and then as the mist slowly cleared, they both saw, reflected in the mirror, that last terrible scene of Zohreh's life. They saw Kassim and Zohreh arguing. The nobleman threw the old woman to the ground and told her he was going to destroy her and all her family. His cruel hawk face twisted with demonic fury as Zohreh cursed him, then he whirled on the defenceless old woman and brought his sword down with appalling force. Blood instantly spurted from Zohreh's neck as it was sliced right through, and her head flew off. Khaled and Soheila were both sobbing by this time, gripping each other tightly. The Talisman had fallen to the floor between them. But they could not look away as Kassim calmly wiped the blood off his sword and kicked the old woman's body as if she were a dog. They saw the self-satisfied smile on his face. Khaled groaned. This evil man was his ancestor: his blood ran in Khaled's veins, as Zohreh's ran in Soheila's. He could feel nothing but despair and horror, could think nothing but that maybe he did deserve to be punished, just for being born . . .

But then Soheila spoke. She had picked up the Talisman and was holding it again. There were tears running down her face but her voice was steady as she said, 'Grandmother of Grandmothers, you have been avenged. The evil man died in torment and his spirit is now in Jehannem, where he will be for all eternity. His memory is reviled in his family; not even his grave is safe from dishonour. Only ghouls and wild dogs haunt it now.'

The scene in the mirror disappeared and was replaced by their reflections. Soheila's face and form were still shadowy, the ghostly features of her ancestor constantly shading into the girl's own reflection. He saw the ghost's thin lips move, but still couldn't hear what she said.

'I saw it,' answered Soheila, and then she took Khaled's hand. 'So did Khaled. The evil man has been punished long since, Grandmother of Grandmothers. Innocent blood has flowed since then, and it was not that of our family. It is enough, oh Zohreh of the Melkior clan. It is enough. It must end.'

There was silence, then Soheila repeated, 'It must end, oh Zohreh of the Melkior clan, revered ancestor. Will you give Khaled and I your blessing to go to the Emerald Mountain of Kaf to ask the Recorder to efface the curse? Will you remember the way of the Truth-teller, who bids us to forgive our enemies if justice has been done? Oh, Zohreh of the Melkior clan, the way of our ancestors was tempered with mercy as well as wrath. You see that we have found our family's dearest treasure, and that its light falls on Khaled as well as on me. Let that be your guide, sweet Grandmother of Grandmothers. Let your spirit be at rest. Let it go quietly into the peace of Akamenia, now you know the evil man has been punished, for all time.' Her voice became more urgent. 'Will you give us your blessing? Will you tell us the way to the Emerald Mountain?'

Khaled cast a quick glance at the clock. It was almost fifteen minutes past the hour. He looked at the skyflower. Its petals were drooping. Kareen had warned them it might be dangerous once the flower faded – that even the good power of the Talisman might not protect Khaled if the old woman's spirit stayed vengeful. Fear rose up inside him but he quickly pushed it back. He musn't be afraid. He must trust Soheila, and he must hold fast to her.

The girl's face was bathed in sweat. Her eyes were staring, her voice low and desperate. Khaled knew she was at the end of her tether, and still the ghost had not answered her plea. Khaled knew then that he must act. His hand lightly on the Talisman, he spoke for the first time.

'Only guilty blood pays for the shedding of innocent blood,' he said clearly. 'Zohreh of the Melkior clan, I, Khaled bin Abdullah al-Farouk, descendant of the wicked Kassim, do pledge this to you and to your descendants: that we will pay in full all we owe, and will do everything in our power to restore the honour and memory of your family, and yourself. The truth shall be told, in every corner of this land, and Parsari, and Kassim's wicked lies shall be exposed. This I promise, with all my heart and my soul.'

Soheila looked at him, her face filled with light. 'Khaled and I stand together, today and forever,' she said firmly, as the quarter-hour began to strike. 'Whatever happens, Zohreh of the Melkior clan, we will live henceforth as if the curse had no power.' And she held Khaled's hand, over the Talisman.

It was then that she heard, in her mind, the ghost's last words. 'The Emerald Mountain is not hard to find: it is in your heart, my child. The curse is ended this night. Pray for me, Soheila of the Melkior clan; pray for me that my spirit be at rest and find peace in the bosom of Akamenia. Bless you, my child, for your courage and your strength, for doing what had to be done.' Faintly then, the ghost whispered, 'And peace be upon the house of Khaled al-Farouk, whose heart is great and whose courage matches your own. Peace be upon you both, my children, for the curse of Zohreh is at an end.'

Soheila looked at Khaled. The same glowing expression was on his face. She knew that somehow he had heard and understood the last words of her ancestor, Zohreh, whose spirit would no longer haunt this place.

The face in the mirror was now Soheila's own. Suddenly, a lump came into her throat. Zohreh had gone — gone beyond the ken of mortals, gone into the mysterious realms beyond time. She hoped that Akamenia would indeed receive her into the peace of his being.

'Soheila,' whispered Khaled, his eyes on her face, 'Soheila, did you mean what you said, about us standing together, now and forever?'

A flush mounted up her neck, but she nodded. His smile told her how he felt.

Soheila said hurriedly, 'We must still reach the

Emerald Mountain, Khaled, now Zohreh has given us her blessing to do so.'

'Yes, we must,' he said. 'How do we get there?'

'I think we must call in the others, Khaled. Will you fetch them?'

He nodded. They squeezed each others' hands, then Khaled was gone, running to get his father and the others. They rushed in, talking in relief, their faces slowly uncreasing from the worry. Soheila stood there, her gaze still on the mirror. She could not yet think clearly about what she had felt and experienced this night, but she knew that she was utterly changed. Now there was hope where there had been despair, and sweet delight where once there had been endless night. Her tears for Zohreh's cruel fate would not end, but they would not be tears of bitterness any more. The future would not forget the past, but the future would not be held hostage to the past, or nothing could ever change.

They stood together in the library, all of them.

Soheila spoke solemnly. 'Place your hand on the Talisman of the Star, Khaled. Now, together, we will call on the Recorder of the Emerald Mountain. We will travel there in our hearts, and we will ask her to end the curse, as my ancestor Zohreh wants. Never again, my dearest friend, will there be bitterness and sorrow between your family and mine.'

And as the others watched in delight and awe, Khaled placed his hand on the box and Soheila put hers on top of his. Each felt the jolt of contact, the warmth that instantly flowed, the piercing joy that rushed into both of them. It seemed that in the place where their fingers met on the Talisman a vision grew: a vision of a beautiful green mountain wreathed in mist. They looked at each other, saw the same vision reflected in each other's eyes, and smiled. They knew at that moment that there would be respect and honour between their families – and much more. There would be true friendship of the heart, a love as deep as it was sweet. And one day, the families would be joined, through them.

'Let us speak these words,' said Soheila, and she said, 'Oh, Recorder, we ask you, in Zohreh's name, to end the curse on this house. It is Zohreh's wish that the sorrow and bitterness be ended forever, and her spirit be allowed to rest. We ask you this as a daughter of the house of Zohreh, and a son of the house of Kassim.'

Khaled repeated them, then with Soheila.

Solemnly it was said, but with great joy – and that joy was also in the hearts and minds of all who watched them. Then it seemed to everyone in the room that a figure appeared between the two children – a figure tall and flickering as a white flame, with a veiled face, and a book in one hand and a long quill in the other. They felt a sense of great power, of a power that was as mighty as it was good. The veiled face bent over the book, the quill wrote, and a ghostly voice intoned these words: 'It is done. The curse of Zohreh is ended.' The figure rose to its full height, flickered once, then was gone. Only the echo of its words remained, hanging on the still air.

Epilogue

Mahmoud was not caught by the Prince's investigators. He had vanished utterly. An alert was put out for him, but he evaded all checkpoints and frontier posts. Though the kidnappers' camp was searched, the bodies of the other men and the cars were too badly burnt to provide any form of identification.

The Mesomian ambassador was summoned by the Prince of Ameerat to explain the whole incident, but he refused to accept any responsibility or knowledge of anything. Indeed, he became angry and impatient at the mere idea. 'Why are you seeking to impute to Mesomia the evil plots of kidnappers whose nationality is not even known?' the Ambassador said haughtily.

The Prince had no choice but to let the matter slide. The only other option was to provoke a full-scale international diplomatic incident, and everyone knew The Vampire would use that as an excuse to go to war.

Ameerat most certainly did not want war with its huge and dangerous neighbour.

The Shayk would have liked to hammer the Mesomians but he was forced to admit that there was little the Prince could do in the circumstances. Besides, as Gur Thalab had flown away on the carpet to seek the Enchantress who had woven it, and find his own destiny, it was quite clear that the Mesomians would have little interest in the al-Farouks any more.

For it seemed to be the carpet they had been after, probably for the same reasons as Gur Thalab had been so excited to discover its true nature. Perhaps they had known about its deeper message and had somehow tracked it all the way from the Marshlands it had been stolen from. Or perhaps they had simply followed Khaled and Husam back from the Carpet Bazaar because they wanted to know how and why a wealthy Ameeratan family had obtained a Mesomian magic carpet.

In any case, there was a great deal else to think about in the palace of the al-Farouks these days. As soon as possible, a messenger had been sent trekking into the mountains of Parsari to deliver a message to a modest house in the village of Sholeh. There, a poor couple and their son, who had wept every tear in their heads for their vanished daughter and sister, Soheila, discovered, for the first time in their lives, the meaning of happiness and hope. In a very short time they would be on their way to Jumana to be reunited with Soheila, and to seal the end of the curse of Zohreh and the beginning of a new day for the Melkior clan.

It would be a momentous meeting, for it would close the circle that had begun a century ago, when Zohreh the Akamenian had so fatefully set foot in the city of Jumana. Many celebrations and feasts were planned and the palace was in uproar, with the gossip coming out of the servants' quarters reaching great levels of frenzy. According to Ismail – who, newly promoted to apprentice chef, had by now been let into nearly all the secrets – Soheila and Khaled were to be betrothed at this meeting. He was pleased to see that no-one contradicted him, only blushed and looked at each other with a little smile.

Husam and Kareen would be staying for the festivities, of course. Now the shadows had lifted from the palace they were enjoying themselves. Husam went out on hunting trips into the desert with his old friend the Shayk. And his red-headed companion had been seen by some of the House-Jinn heading towards the Fountain of the Skyflowers, and the company of Ebon Zarah. Many of the House-Jinn breathed a sigh of relief at her absence; she was altogether too spiky and difficult and uninhibited a spirit for them to ever feel comfortable around. Only two missed her and waited for her return with anything like impatience, if such a term can be used of immortals. Hamarajol, the Bathroom-Jinn, missed the gossip and bustle and general topsy-turvying that Kareen had brought with her.

And Farasha, of the Repository of Forgotten Books, missed her too, though he would have been hard put to say why. In recent days, his domain had been freshly painted, shelves constructed in it, the dull books taken out of their boxes and honourably displayed on them, and a formula dedicated to him painted above the doorway of his domain. There was a sense within the House-Jinn caste that he had most definitely been promoted in the hierarchy, and Bikaj himself had condescended to pay him a personal visit and examine the new conditions in his domain. But for some reason, Farasha felt an odd restlessness. On certain nights, very late, when no-one, human or Jinn, was stirring in the house, he crept out of his fine domain towards the smelly realm of Hamarajol. There, hovering a little anxiously above the doorjamb, he would have long, circular conversations with the sardonic bathroom spirit and the Alhindi Jinn master Sharib, who had also stayed on in the palace. And then the restlessness would fade, and the little Moth-Jinn would be unaccountably happy, and return to his Repository quite refreshed, very pleased with himself and the whole world.

Glossary

Adhubilah – a sacred formula in the language of Al Aksara giving protection against evil spirits such as afreets. Usually written up above doors.

Akamenian – the ancient religion of Parsari until the Mujisal conquerors came. Most Parsarians are now Mujisals but a few cling to the old religion. In modern times Akamenians have suffered persecution by the Parsarian Government and fanatics. The religion takes its name from the name of the Akamenians' God, Akamenia, who is often represented as a pillar of fire, and sometimes as a burning star. The prophet of the Akamenians, the Truthteller, wrote the sacred book The Realm of Akamenia. Astronomy is very important to the Akamenians and their high priests, the Magvandas, study the paths of the stars very closely.

Al Aksara – the Great Desert. This huge peninsula is the heartland of Dawtarn el 'Jisal. The Mujisal religion began in Al Aksara, as did the Aksaran language, in which the Book of Light is written. Its most sacred site is the House of Light, in the great city of Umalkurrah, in the kingdom of Riyaldaw. It was here the Messenger, prophet of the Mujisals, lived, and it is also here that the Heaven Stone is kept. Al Aksara, whose economy in modern times is built on oil, gold, banking, and trading, is dominated by the vast oil-rich kingdom of Riyaldaw, but also includes many smaller countries, such as the principality of Ameerat. To the north, Al Aksara has land borders with Mesomia, Masrikhan and Levantian. To the north-east, across the Gulf of Parsari, lies Parsari; to the west, across the Narrow Sea, lie Faraona and Aswadd; and to the south lies the great ocean, the Shining Sea. Aksaran is spoken in all these countries except Parsari.

Albalhol – mythical monster from the deserts of Faraona who in ancient times was reputed to lie in wait for lone travellers and ask them riddles; if they could not answer, the monster ate them. Albalhol was finally turned into stone by a magician-prince, and this stone monster can still be seen near the ancient Royal Tombs at Teban in the Faraonan desert.

Alhind – huge country to the south of Al Aksara. It has a Dharbudsu majority, and Mujisal, Nashranee and Akamenian minorities. Once a very rich and powerful empire, over the centuries it has grown poorer, though it is still a force to be reckoned with. There are many Alhindis working in the oil-rich countries of Al Aksara.

The Alhindis are renowned for their magical skills and their cleverness. Jinn mastery is a particularly Alhindi skill.

Afreet – powerful evil Jinn, usually living in Jehannem under the rule of Iblis. May also be enslaved by human sorcerers and used to accomplish difficult tasks.

Ameerat – the principality of Ameerat is a small but wealthy country of Al Aksara. Its capital city, Jumana, is the richest in the region, and the centre of the gold trade. As well as Jumana, there are three other large cities in Ameerat, but much of the country is desert, camel farms and date-palm oases. The head of the government is the Prince, who rules as a hereditary monarch, with a council of noblemen, each the head of great families. Abdullah al-Farouk is one of the Prince's councillors. There are people from all over the world living and working in the cities of Ameerat. Tribal nomads still roam the desert, though they have become less warlike than they were in the past.

Arga – traditional title for a prince of the green Kirtis Mountains in the north of Mesomia.

Aswadd – large country to the west of Al Aksara. Most Aswaddis are Mujisal, though there are also many Aswaddi Nashranees as well.

Dawtarn el 'Jisal – The countries in the world that have a majority Mujisal population are known collectively as Dawtarn el 'Jisal, or Lands of the Mujisals.

Dharbudsu – once the majority religion in Jayangan, until

the advent of the Mujisal religion. Its sacred writings are contained within the Book of Life. Some countries in the world, such as Alhind, are still dominated by the Dharbudsu religion. These are known collectively as 'Dawtarn el 'Budsu', or Lands of Dharbudsu.

Dhow – a type of wooden Aksaran trading ship that has sails but also, these days, an engine. It is used for short trips, such as across the Gulf of Parsari.

Ebon Zarah – a Jinn who is the spirit of the Fountain of the Skyflowers, a beautiful oasis in Ameerat. Unlike many Jinn, he has the power to speak to the dead.

Emerald Mountain of Kaf – a mystical spirit-mountain that exists outside of time and space. It is the realm of the powerful Jinn known as the Recorder.

Faraona – a large kingdom to the west of Al Aksara, across the Shining Sea. Faraona has a very long history. Centuries ago it was a very powerful empire that stretched into Al Aksara and beyond. Relics of this once-great empire, such as the stone monster Albalhol, and the Royal Tombs at Teban, remain.

House of Light – the most sacred place in Dawtarn el 'Jisal, where the Messenger gave his first teachings, and where the Heaven Stone, token of God's love, is kept in a sacred shrine. The House of Light is in the capital city of Riyaldaw, Umalkurrah, and every year hundreds of thousands of Mujisals make a pilgrimage there.

Ghoul – a type of evil Jinn that haunts graveyards and cemeteries. Ghouls are flesh-eaters and are very dangerous. Like all Jinns, they are shapeshifters, and can present themselves as beautiful women. They also manifest as hyenas and other scavengers.

Iblis – Lord of the evil Jinn. His realm is Jehannem, place of torment and eternal fire.

Jayangan – an island far to the east of Al Aksara. In Jayanganese, the name of the island means 'dwelling place of the gods'.

Jehannem – the realm of Iblis, lord of the evil Jinn. A place of torment and eternal fire.

Jinn – one of the Hidden People or spirit people of Al Aksara and many other places in the Dawtarn el 'Jisal. Jinns can be good or bad or in-between, male or female in appearance, or even present as animals. They can metamorphose at will and have various magical powers. They were created from fire and are immortal. Some live in tribes and clans, others are lone spirits.

Jinn master – a type of magician from Alhind who is able to make minor Jinn perform useful tasks. Jinn masters are forbidden to use bad magic, so they are not regarded as sorcerers.

Kalfkat – a small saltbush that grows in the northern deserts of Al Aksara. Known as the 'herb of forgetfulness', its leaves can be dried, powdered and made into a stupefying concoction that gives a similar effect to drinking wine. The leaves can also be dried and smoked.

Kirtis Mountains – high mountainous region in the north of Mesomia. Kirtis is very different from much of

Mesomia, for instead of being flat, hot and dry, it is a
region of green pastures, small stone villages, rushing
streams, deep oak forests and high snowy slopes. The
Kirtis people are not Aksaran. They have their own
language, and though they are mainly Mujisals, there are
also Nashranees and Akamenians amongst them. They
are renowned as fighters and singers.

Magvanda – high priest in the Akamenian religion. As
well as officiating at religious ceremonies, the Magvandas study the stars. The Magvanda priesthood is not
hereditary.

Masrikhan – country to the north of Al Aksara, bordering
Mesomia as well. It is famous for its lace and roses.

Mesomia – country to the north of Ameerat. Its capital,
Madinatu es Salam, was once the seat of powerful kings,
and a place of great learning and culture. Mesomia is
now under the direct dictatorship of a ruthless tyrant
called Haroun bin Said al-Alakah, better known as The
Vampire, who murdered the last king and seized power
decades ago. The Vampire is a ruthless oppressor and has
a feared secret police force who have killed thousands
of Mesomians. The Vampire is also reputed to have evil
magical powers, which keep his people in thrall.

Messenger – the great prophet of the Mujisals.

Mujisal – the majority religion of many countries in the
world, including Al Aksara, where it originated. Its sacred
writings are contained in the Book of Light. A small
section of the Mujisal population practises the

'Pumujisal' variety of the religion, which is much stricter than the general variety. The countries in the world that have a majority Mujisal population are known collectively as Dawtarn el 'Jisal, or Lands of the Mujisals.

Nashranee – one of the world's great religions. Though it is a minority religion in the countries of the Dawtarn el 'Jisal, it is a majority religion in many other places, such as the Rummiyan Empire. Countries where this religion is practised are collectively known as 'Dawtarn el 'Ranee', or Lands of the Nashranees. Its sacred writings are contained in the Book of Love.

Parsari – large country to the north-east of Ameerat, over the Parsari Gulf. Like Alhind and Faraona, Parsari was once a mighty empire. These days it is still a very important country but it has become quite poor. It had a hereditary emperor until a few years ago a fiery Pumujisal preacher overthrew him and became ruler. Parsari has been at war with Mesomia many times. Unlike most countries in the region, Parsari is not inhabited by people of Aksaran origin. It was once dominated by the Akamenian religion, which originated there, but has been Mujisal for centuries now.

Pumujisal – small, strict sect of the Mujisal religion. Frowns on pleasure of all sorts, believes in work and study only. Its adherents usually dress in pure white, and are often opposed to other religions.

Riyaldaw – vast desert kingdom bordering Ameerat. It is a vastly wealthy country due to oil exports and pilgrimage tithes. It is not as peaceful as Ameerat, with rebels in the south and north seeking to overthrow the royal family. Its capital city, Umalkurrah, is the most holy city in all of the Mujisal world, and the House of Light is located there.

Sambuk – a type of large Parsarian wooden sailing ship.

Shayk – honorific Al Aksaran title for a great nobleman, meaning 'lord'.

Shining Ones – another name for angels, who are made of light and are messengers of God.

Truthteller – the prophet of the Akamenians, who arose thousands of years ago to proclaim the message of Akamenia.

Zummiyah water – water taken from the sacred well near the House of Light in Al Aksara. Can protect against evil spirits.

About the author

Sophie Masson was born in Indonesia of French parents and was brought up mainly in Australia. A bilingual French and English speaker, she has a master's degree in French and English literature. Sophie is the prolific author of numerous young adult fantasy novels as well as several adult novels. She lives in Armidale, New South Wales, with her husband and children.

Acknowledgements

The author wishes to acknowledge the support of the May Gibbs Children's Literature Trust, in whose Adelaide studio *The Curse of Zohreh* was first planned and sketched out.

Thanks also to Dr Raghid Nahhas, who gave me Farasha's name and set me on the way to creating a favourite character.

SNOW, FIRE, SWORD

Sophie Masson

Don't Miss

SNOW, FIRE, SWORD

Book One in *The Chronicles of El Jisal*

Extract from *Snow, Fire, Sword*

One

How tiring this journey was! Why did they have to walk, rather than go by car or bus? Why go around the long way rather than use the main roads? Why, oh why, spend uncomfortable nights sleeping in forests and ditches instead of comfortable guesthouses? Grumbling to himself, Adi trudged along the muddy dirt track behind his master. Before they left, he'd been so excited at the prospect of his first visit to Kotabunga, the great capital city of Jayangan. It was more than excitement at the prospect of seeing the city, seat of the Sultan of Jayangan. It was also because this was a great moment in Adi's life.

After two years in Empu Wesiagi's workshop, working at all kinds of tasks, Adi had been allowed to help his master create an important new kris, from beginning to almost the end: carefully shaping and tempering the curved skystone blade, decorating the metal and leather scabbard with delicate tracework. Only right at the end did Empu Wesiagi take over, for that was the time when the sacred, magic formulae were said over the weapon to dedicate its spirit to its new owner, who was to be none other than the Sultan himself!

Adi's joy at this honour had been tempered by the kris-smith's strange insistence that he not tell anyone where they were going. If he must tell his family something, he should tell them they were going over the sea to Balian Besakih, to consult with a kris-smith over there. Adi could not understand this deceit but he trusted his master so did as he was told. After all, Empu Wesiagi had given him the coveted apprentice-ship in his workshop, and had over the last couple of years proven to be a good and kind master. Yes, Empu Wesiagi must have his reasons.

As he must have his reasons for choosing to go to Kotabunga by these winding and out-of-the-way paths. It didn't help, though, when you felt tired and dirty and uncomfortable, when the road seemed to stretch interminably in front of . . .

'Stop!' Empu Wesiagi's voice jolted Adi out of his rebellious thoughts. 'Adi, can you hear anything?'

Adi stared at his master, who had stopped stock still in the middle of the path. The old man's face was pinched and drawn. He looked unwell, thought Adi, dismayed.

'Hear anything, sir?' he said carefully. There was nothing of note to be heard, just the usual sounds of the countryside – the breeze swishing in the paddy fields to either side of the road, the shushing sound of wind in the forest beyond, bird calls, distant engine noises. He looked around. Night was beginning to fall, shadows were creeping in over the fields, it would soon be time to stop and . . . In the next instant, Adi got the shock of his life, for his beloved master sprang on him with such ferocity that he fell over backwards onto the muddy road. Before he had time to react, Empu Wesiagi pulled him with extraordinary force deep into the paddy. 'Stay here!' he ordered. Dazed, baffled, Adi tried to scramble to his feet. With a swift movement, the kris-maker unsheathed the kris – the beautiful new weapon that was a gift to the Sultan – and pointed it threateningly at his apprentice, who fell back. 'Stay here. Don't even try to argue. Whatever you see, whatever you hear, whatever happens, don't move, or you will die.'

Adi could well believe it. His master's eyes shone with a red light; the kris's beautifully made, sinuous, wickedly sharp blade was pointed right at Adi's throat.

'Do you understand me, Adi?'

Adi swallowed. He nodded. Empu Wesiagi's eyes narrowed. He reached into his clothes and took out two lengths of rope and a large handkerchief. 'I have to do this, Adi. You cannot follow me.' Kneeling down, he swiftly tied Adi's hands together, and then his feet. But before he could gag the boy with the cloth, Adi suddenly found his voice. 'Master, why are you doing this? What have I done wrong?'

'Forgive me,' said Empu Wesiagi, tying the gag around Adi's mouth. 'It is for your own safety. The hantumu must not know you are with me.'

The engine noise was getting louder. No, not one engine, but several motorbike engines. An ordinary sound — so why did the hair rise on the back of Adi's head, why did his spine feel like ice? He could not speak, but he could still think, and in his mind, two words spoken by the kris-maker echoed. The hantumu. He shot a look at his master. Was the great Empu Wesiagi in league with the hantumu?

Empu Wesiagi whispered, 'Adi, there is no time. But do not forget this. I brought you with me because you are the very best apprentice I have ever had. And that is why I cannot afford to let the hantumu know you are with me. Adi. You must get to Kotabunga.'

Adi closed his eyes. His heart pounded, his bound hands were clammy. He was in a dream. A nightmare. None of this was happening. When he opened his eyes again, his master had vanished. He heard the swishing sounds the paddy grass made as the old kris-maker ran swiftly back to the road. The motorbike engines got louder and louder. Sweat ran down his face, trickled down his neck, soaked his clothes.

Images filled his mind, images cobbled together from overheard stories. The hantumu. Dark forces, figures of whispered legend, of bad dream, and yet now roaming the land once more. The hantumu were eyeless, some said; they dressed all in black and were mounted on black motorbikes, huge swords by their sides. They were assassins but no-one knew where they came from, why they did what they did – murders, kidnappings, the torching of houses, of sacred places. So many things like that had happened in Jayangan in the last few years. No-one had been able to catch them for they always vanished as mysteriously as they had come.

The noise of their engines was so loud now Adi knew they must be only a short distance away; they must be nearly at the spot where he and his master . . . Then suddenly, Empu Wesiagi shouted, 'I am here, you scum. Here, if you can take me! Ah, you thought I would be afraid!'

The motorbikes revved, then were quiet. A cold voice that sent shivers down Adi's spine answered, 'It is nothing to us if you are afraid or not, old man. You come to our master alive or you come to him dead – that is of little importance.'

Adi's heart swelled. His master was most definitely not a traitor.

'You won't take me easily, scum of the devil!' Empu Wesiagi's voice rang out, then a clash of steel.

Adi could imagine the old man standing on guard, surrounded by the evil hantumu. He could imagine him whirling around, attacking them with the new kris he'd made. Empu Wesiagi was a good fighter, as well as a good smith. He would not give up easily.

The battle raged for longer than one would have thought possible knowing that an old man, though strong and broad and big and wily, was gravely out-numbered by evil assassins armed to the teeth. Clash of steel, shouts, screams, bloodcurdling shrieks filled the air for quite some minutes. Bound, gagged, Adi raged against his helplessness, wishing with all his heart he could break his bonds and go and help his master, no matter what he had said. But the rope was tied tightly, the gag too. There was nothing he could do but listen helplessly. His eyes filled with angry tears. Finally came the sound of a motorbike starting up, and another, and another, and another. Four of them. There had been four of them. Adi could hear nothing now except the roar of the machines. An icy hand gripped his heart. Was his master dead, or wounded? Would they come looking for him? No, they did not know he was here. His master had sacrificed himself so they would not know.

The engines rose to a crescendo, then began to fade. Night had fallen. There was no moon. Adi could see nothing. The paddy grass closed in around him, prison and refuge. He had to do as Empu Wesiagi wanted and get to Kotabunga. Yet he was bound and gagged. His master had taken the kris; he could not even cut his bonds. How could he get away?